"I will not share this suite with you!"

Lucille was furious. "There is absolutely no need."

Blair's eyes were wide with anger, too. "For goodness' sake, you ridiculous woman, what does it matter? Why must you be such a prude?"

"I am *not* a prude!" she stormed. "It might not matter to you, but it matters a great deal to me with whom I share a—a room."

"With whom you share a bed, you mean, don't you?" he came back with icy scorn.

"All right, then, yes. With whom I share a bed," she answered.

"I am not asking you to share a bed with me," he said slowly and with insulting emphasis.

Lucille gave in. Something was stirring within her—something she couldn't quite analyze.

Hilda Nickson, a British writer, fell in love with the countryside and the people of East Anglia and the Norfolk Broads on a sailing holiday—a setting she has used in several books. After years of visiting it, she and her husband live in Norfolk, with their own stretch of waterway at the bottom of their garden. As well as sailing, music, drama, bird-watching and gardening are hobbies she enjoys. Her fiftieth book has just been published.

Books by Hilda Nickson

HARLEQUIN ROMANCE
2859—VOYAGE OF DISCOVERY

So Tempting an Offer

Hilda Nickson

Harlequin Books

TORONTO • NEW YORK • LONDON
AMSTERDAM • PARIS • SYDNEY • HAMBURG
STOCKHOLM • ATHENS • TOKYO • MILAN

Original hardcover edition published in 1988
by Mills & Boon Limited

ISBN 0-373-17035-1

Harlequin Romance first edition April 1989

CHAPTER ONE

IT WAS NOT that Lucille disliked men. In general she enjoyed their company, particularly if they were fairly intelligent, liked good music and had a reasonable sense of humour.

But there had been quite a few times when she'd vowed that never again would she allow herself to fall in love with one of them. If a woman smiled at a man it was invariably taken as an encouragement to become familiar in a way she did not like. If she didn't she was considered to be 'playing hard to get' and therefore a challenge. And somehow or other Lucille seemed to attract men without meaning to. Never having considered herself particularly attractive, she was quite unaware of the effect of her smile, her elusive quality when she was serious, the fact that she had an extraordinarily good figure and knew how to dress to her own advantage.

What troubled her at times was that, being no longer a teenager, she always seemed to attract the wrong kind—those who wanted everything except marriage, others who were already married and preferred to stay that way, in spite of the fact that their wives did not understand them and that she, Lucille, was the only woman they had ever really loved. And worse still, the type she most disliked, full of their own importance, who obviously considered themselves to be superior beings and let the world know it.

Like the man who was approaching the reception desk now, for example, thought Lucille, from the other side of it. This was a five-star hotel in the heart of London's West End, and from his general attitude as he glanced

5

around, one would have thought he was the owner of
the place. He was tall, with the aloof, commanding
presence of one who was supremely self-confident. His
well-cut suit of fine material showed a figure which was
firm and straight. She watched him as his gaze ranged
critically around the large foyer.

Then suddenly he looked straight at her, and she knew
a sense of having been caught staring at him. He crossed
the floor, and as he reached the desk she reminded herself
that he was most likely a guest—or going to be.

She smiled automatically. 'Good afternoon, sir.'

His glance flicked critically over her appearance, and
she bristled inwardly.

'And good afternoon to you,' he answered in a deep,
rich voice with an accent she could not quite place. 'I
believe I have a reservation.'

'Your name, sir?' she enquired coolly.

'Gregory. B.S. Gregory.'

Her glance went swiftly down the reservation book.
'Ah, yes. A suite—the Windsor on the first floor.' She
might have known. He was that kind of client; nothing
but the best would do. That suite cost more for one night
than she earned in a week. She passed a registration card
across the counter to him which he rapidly filled in.
'Welcome to the International,' she offered as he passed
it back to her. Had he been a regular, it would have
been: 'Welcome back.'

He gave her the most prolonged and penetrating look
she had ever received from anyone in her life, and for
a split second something very odd happened. It was as
though time slipped. He wasn't a stranger; he was
someone she knew quite well, someone she—— She drew
a sharp breath and gathered her wits together.

'Thank you, sir,' she said in the most businesslike tone
she could muster, yet realising somewhere at the back
of her mind that her tone lacked that faint suggestion

of warmth she had been trained to use towards a hotel guest.

With relief she lowered her gaze sufficiently to read his name and address and to register the fact that he was a British subject. She noticed his writing too, firm and upright. But when she looked up again she found she was still being treated to his scrutiny. She picked up the small bell which would bring along a nearby porter and turned to reach down the key to the man's suite, feeling more ruffled than she had for a very long time. Who did this man think he was, apart from B.S. Gregory, British subject? And what gave him the right to scrutinise her as though she were some kind of curio?

The porter piled the man's expensive luggage on to a trolley, and with yet another penetrating look the new guest turned and followed the porter towards the lift.

'And who on earth was that?' murmured Jim Doyle in her ear.

Lucille turned slowly to her friend and colleague on Reception. 'I really don't know, except that his name is Gregory and he comes from Cambridge.'

'Well, he certainly gave you the once-over! I watched him.' He grinned. 'Not that I blame him.'

She laughed shortly. 'Don't be an idiot!'

'I'm not being an idiot, far from it. Anyway, don't forget you've got a date with me tonight.'

'Of course I won't forget,' she told him. 'What on earth makes you think I might?'

Jim pulled a face. 'Well, from the way that man was looking at you, who knows?'

Lucille gave him a mock-threatening look. 'Wait for me around ten, and don't be late,' she muttered as another guest approached her portion of the reception desk.

She liked Jim Doyle. They had been friends for around five months now, and although she was not in love with him, he had all the qualities she liked in a man—and none of the vices. He was not married and he made no attempt to coerce her into sleeping with him—which she would not do anyway. That was not to say he never kissed her or attempted to make love to her, but he was good fun, they had a great deal in common and a ripening affection for each other.

The next few hours were extremely busy ones as more and more guests arrived to check in. At intervals one or two very smart young women approached the desk asking for Mr Gregory. Lucille made no comment to anyone, but she couldn't help thinking that he appeared to have plenty of girlfriends.

'Do you know, that's the fifth girl who's gone up to the Windsor Suite since six o'clock,' murmured Jim, who never missed a thing, and by now, at nearly nine o'clock, the flow of guests checking in was diminishing.

'A popular man, you might say,' she answered.

'Popular? Use your head, Lucille! He's probably some businessman interviewing applicants for the job of his private secretary or something. You'll notice that no men have gone up.'

Lucille grimaced. 'I never thought of that, but you could be right. And I suppose, if that's so, you *can* assume that the job he's offering is for that of secretary. It couldn't possibly be for some higher post, of course!'

Jim simply grinned at her. 'Watch out, your Women's Lib tendencies are showing! You know perfectly well that women make the best secretaries—simply because they're more conscientious and have a mind for details. Not to mention the fact that they're better-looking. What man in his right mind would want a man for a secretary?'

'Thanks very much for the testimonial,' she answered tartly. 'But most women want to be chosen for a job on their intelligence and qualifications, not because of their looks.'

But it was a good-humoured argument. She and Jim often had these kind of debates, and she knew he often said things to tease or provoke her.

'Anyway,' she added for good measure, 'nothing on earth would induce me to be secretary—private or otherwise—to that man.'

'Wouldn't blame you for that, either,' Jim murmured as he moved to attend to a newcomer.

Lucille raised her eyes to the ceiling, as if she would like to see what was going on in the Windsor Suite. Which of the rather glamorous-looking females would get the job? she wondered. That was, if Jim's assumption was correct.

A quarter of an hour later she saw the latest of the young ladies pass through the revolving glass doors on her way out. Obviously the interviews were at an end.

It was then that the hotel manager approached the reception desk. 'The gentleman in the Windsor Suite would like to see you,' he told Lucille.

She frowned. 'To see me? But why?'

'Do as I ask and go up there, please,' the manager said in a smooth but authoritative tone.

Lucille's eyes sparked. 'My job here is that of receptionist, Mr Ferrari. Why should one of the guests ask to see me in his private suite?'

'Come into my office,' he said, 'and I'll tell you.'

Lucille had no option but to obey, if she wanted to keep her job. She followed the manager into his office.

'Now then,' he said, after closing the door, 'I'm going to tell you something, and I want your word that you'll tell no one else.'

She nodded, wondering what was coming. 'All right, Mr Ferrari, you have my word.'

'Good. Few people know this, and Mr Saunders doesn't wish it to become generally known.'

'And who is Mr Saunders?' she asked, somewhat mystified.

'It's the gentleman in the Windsor Suite who calls himself Gregory.'

Lucille gave a puzzled frown. 'But—but why——'

'If you will stop interrupting and listen, Miss LeFurve, I'll tell you. Mr Saunders is the owner of this hotel— and many others throughout the country.'

She gave a gasp of surprise. 'Good heavens!'

'Yes, good heavens, and he wants to see you. What about, I don't know, but go at once. And don't breathe a word to *anyone*—you understand?'

'Yes. Yes, Mr Ferrari, I understand.'

In something of a daze she made her way up to the first floor. No wonder the man had looked as though he owned the hotel. He *did* own it! But what on earth did he want to see her about? Not to offer her a job as his private secretary, surely? If he did, she would refuse. She was quite happy where she was, and she certainly had no wish to work for *that* man—at least, not in a personal capacity. She glanced at her reflection in one of the gilt mirrors on the first floor, wishing she had not left her handbag in the cupboard downstairs. She didn't want to impress this man particularly, all the same she liked to look her best when meeting anyone for the first time like this. She sighed. There was nothing she could do about her appearance now, anyway. Her lipstick was intact, she noticed, even if her face could have done with a touch of powder. As for the grey suit she was wearing—— Lucille pulled a wry face. It bore no comparison with the glamorous clothes of the girls she had seen being directed to the Windsor Suite. But then, she told herself, she did not consider herself to be in competition with any of them. She was *not* going to be his secretary, even if the job was offered.

She took a deep breath and knocked on the door of the suite. She turned the knob tentatively, waiting to be bidden to enter, but suddenly the knob was wrenched from her grasp, the door was flung open and she found herself face to face with the man she had come to see.

The close proximity quite unnerved her. He was hand-somer than she had at first thought. He had changed out of his tailored suit and was wearing a loose-fitting lounging jacket in deep wine-coloured velvet under which was a white silk shirt open at the neck.

'Ah, yes, Miss LeFurve,' he said smoothly. 'Do come in and sit down.'

Lucille advanced into the room, giving him a suspicious, sidelong glance. What was he up to? Was she really going to be interviewed for another job, or—or——

'A drink, Miss LeFurve?'

There was no time for her to consider possible alternatives for his inviting her into his suite.

'Er—a sherry—a medium sherry,' she answered, sitting down, but carefully avoiding the elegant settee. She had no trust in him whatsoever, and had no intention of giving him the chance to sit down beside her.

He placed a glass of pale gold sherry on the small table beside her chair along with an elegant little bowl filled with a variety of nuts. He then seated himself opposite her and surveyed her in silence for a minute or two. Lucille sipped her drink and found it delicious, but avoided his gaze.

At last he asked, 'Miss LeFurve, how long have you been with the firm?'

'I would have thought you'd know, as I'm told you're the owner of this group of hotels,' she answered pertly, though for the life of her she didn't know what had made her make such a reply.

She saw his jaw tighten and his eyes narrow to slits. 'If I'd known I wouldn't have asked you,' he told her in a steely voice. 'I don't attempt to keep tabs on all my employees—I leave that to my managers. You couldn't have been here very long. You weren't here when last I came to the hotel about six months ago.'

Lucille recovered herself. 'No. No, I'm sorry. I've been here about five months.'

His face relaxed. She tried to guess his age, but it was difficult. Not too young. Mature, but certainly not middle-aged.

'And what were you doing before that?' he enquired.

Lucille put down her glass. 'Mr Saunders, before I answer any more questions, may I ask why you've invited me up here to see you?'

His dark brows raised a fraction. 'You're very direct, for a receptionist, Miss LeFurve.'

She felt the colour infuse her cheeks. Was there implied criticism here?

'I'm—sorry,' she said for the second time. 'But I *am* very curious as to why you wanted to see me.'

There was a moment's silence. She noticed that he did not smoke, neither was he drinking, so that he indulged in none of the usual artifices for bridging a gap or considering what he should say next. He just sat there, one hand resting on the arm of his chair, the other fingering his chin, the most composed man she had ever met. She found herself wishing she could control her own feelings better, and wondering what it was about him which made her react so much against him. Was it simply his self-assurance? Of course, in his position he could afford——

'All right,' he said decisively, 'I'll tell you—if you'll promise not to make an immediate move towards the door. I—had hoped to talk to you more, to get to know you a little better first. However——'

'First?' she asked suspiciously. 'First before what?'

'Patience, Miss LeFurve, patience! I asked you to come to see me because I have it in mind to offer you a job—a different one from that of receptionist. I wanted, first, to talk to you, naturally, and to get to know you a little. However——'

Lucille got to her feet. Jim was right; he was looking for a new secretary. 'I'm sorry, Mr Saunders, but I'm quite happy where I am, thanks.'

'Sit down, Miss LeFurve—if you please,' he added rather as an afterthought. 'I haven't finished.'

There was a note of authority in his voice which she could not ignore. She sat down again, the thought registering in the back of her mind that he was, after all, her employer already. All the same——

'What—what is the nature of the job you're offering me, Mr Saunders?' she asked, feeling somewhat subdued, but ready to spring up again if goaded.

'If you'll possess your soul in a little patience and listen without interruption, I'll tell you,' he said calmly. 'I'm thinking of expanding—going into Europe, or even further. I have my agents overseas, of course, who've been keeping an eye open for possibilities, but I prefer to see things for myself. I want someone to travel with me, someone who can speak one or two languages fairly fluently, who can take notes and compile reports, and, of course, someone who is free to go abroad, say, for six months or more. I've been looking through the dossier on you, Miss LeFurve, and it seems to me that you fill the bill quite nicely. You're not married—so many smart, young-looking women are nowadays—you speak a number of languages, and if I may say so, you have a certain—poise—which I think essential.'

He paused. Under cover of sipping her sherry Lucille tried to marshal her thoughts. The job sounded intriguing, even exciting. She had always wanted to travel, and had already visited a number of different countries on holidays. But the short stays had always seemed woefully inadequate. And until now, a post overseas had not been possible because of her mother, who had not had very good health and was alone except for Lucille. Now her mother had married again and her health had greatly improved. All the same, her thoughts went on, if this man expected her to jump at the chance the moment it was offered, he was mistaken.

'It sounds very interesting, Mr Saunders,' she said, trying to keep her voice nonchalant. 'It's true that I'm free to make up my own mind, but I do have friends here who will—or rather would——'

'Are you engaged? That, of course, would not be in your dossier.'

'No, it wouldn't.'

There was another pause, then he said pointedly, 'You haven't answered my question. Are you or are you not engaged to be married?'

'Does it matter?' she countered, needled by his persistence.

He took a deep breath as if gathering together his patience. 'For my purpose, yes, it does. Fiancés have a habit of behaving and reacting much the same as husbands—and I wouldn't want any interruption on this undertaking. I want at least six months of concentrated work.'

'With no time off?'

'I didn't say that.' There was a decidedly steely glint in his eyes, and Lucille wondered fleetingly why he was being so patient with her. Had all the other girls he had interviewed been so unsuitable for his requirement? He continued, 'Of course you would have time off, but not a holiday until the job was finished. You said just now that you were free to make your own decisions. If you meant that, and there would be no fiancé demanding your return precipitously or you rushing back home before the job was finished, then we can discuss matters like salary and allowances. You would naturally have an allowance for extra clothes.'

Lucille liked it more and more. She was interested in clothes and liked to dress well. She gave a little secret smile. He had said nothing about the possibility of a fiancé or boyfriend going out to wherever she and her employer might happen to be. Jim might take it into his head to join her at some period for a holiday. What would Mr Saunders have to say then?

'It's beginning to sound quite attractive, Mr Saunders,' she said smoothly.

His lips curved into a sarcastic smile. 'I thought it might. I'd also double the salary you're getting now.'

Her eyes widened slowly. This was a very handsome inducement indeed! What would he expect of her for that kind of money plus a dress allowance? There must be a catch in it somewhere. And more important, what would he be like to work for?

'Money isn't everything, Mr Saunders,' she demurred.

'That's not a very intelligent remark, Miss LeFurve. One doesn't get very far without it.'

She coloured at his rebuke, but registered his opinion as being quite worldly.

'Nevertheless, it expresses what I mean,' she answered doggedly. 'It's very good of you to offer me such a well-paid position, but I'm not sure that I should accept.'

'Why not?'

'Well, I don't quite know what it entails, for one thing.'

'And for another?' he prompted as she paused.

'Two other reasons, really. I—don't really know you well enough, and—and I have friends here who will miss me over such a long period. I really am perfectly happy where I am.'

She saw his jaw tighten as she spoke. He was not a man to be crossed. Suppose he said to her, 'You either do this job or none at all for my firm'? Where would she be then? Unemployed. Good jobs were becoming scarce; it might take her a long time to get another. And although he normally left the hiring and firing to his managers, it was still his prerogative and he would do so, she guessed, if occasion demanded it.

Suddenly, in spite of all the pros and cons, she knew she wanted this job. Every nerve and muscle in her body tightened as she waited for him to speak, to perhaps issue the ultimatum.

She was ready to scream when at last he said, 'I've already told you what the job entails. Six months or so of travel, staying in specific hotels, using your observation, mixing with people to ascertain their views, writing reports and so on. I'll give you until—lunch time tomorrow to think it over and give me your answer.' He rose to his feet, indicating that the interview was over. 'Come to my suite at one o'clock tomorrow.'

It was more of a command than a request. Having half a mind to refuse right now, Lucille rose and moved towards the door. With rapid strides he was there before her to open it. She thanked him and caught a whiff of his aftershave—and something else: an indefinable, lingering scent of his masculinity.

'You'd be well advised to think over my offer very carefully, Miss LeFurve,' was his parting shot.

It sounded almost like a threat. Lucille half turned to tell him he could keep his job, but she had already stepped over the threshold and he was closing the door.

She took a few steps along the wide corridor, then paused and let out an angry breath. Damn the man! The job sounded so tempting. A dress allowance, double her present salary—and an opportunity to travel into the bargain. But could she put up with him for six months or more?

She glanced at her watch. She would be off duty in a few minutes and Jim would be waiting for her. She gathered together her composure and remembered that she had been asked by the manager not to tell anyone that 'Mr Gregory' in the Windsor Suite was, in actual fact, Mr Saunders, the owner of the hotel. She would have to tell Jim about the offer, of course. How would he take it? They were not engaged or anything, but——

The night staff had already taken over when she went downstairs, and Jim was waiting for her in the foyer. She collected her handbag and joined him.

'And what was it all about, then?' he asked at once.

'I'll tell you later. Let's go now.'

Jim's car was at the back of the hotel and they made their way there.

'Was it a job?' Jim persisted.

'Yes.'

'As his secretary?'

'Something like that.'

'And are you going to take it?'

Lucille felt a sudden impatience with his questioning such as she had never felt before.

'For goodness' sake, Jim, stop asking so many questions! I haven't had time to think about it yet.'

'All right, all right, keep your hair on!' he came back. 'There's no need to be so touchy about it. You obviously didn't say no to him.'

Lucille did not answer. She was beginning to wish she had not arranged to have Jim to a late supper at her flat. She could have done with being alone so that she could think. She had only between now and one o'clock tomorrow in which to make up her mind. Jim would probably not leave until around midnight, and tomorrow spent largely at the reception desk would not give her much time for private thoughts. One part of her mind wanted to accept the job—it was a tremendous offer, and nine women out of ten would have had no hesitation in accepting at once. Why did she, simply because she did not like the boss? she asked herself. After all, if the job did not turn out well, she could always give in her notice and come home again. He surely wouldn't expect her to enter into a binding contract for the next six months. Her present agreement was a month's notice on either side.

Jim drew up outside her flat, and she realised she had not spoken to him for the rest of their five-minute journey.

'Drink?' she asked as she switched on the lights of her flat.

'Thanks.'

He crossed to the small table where she kept her modest supply of drinks, and she went into the bedroom to change out of her suit as she always did. Often she would slip into a long wrap-around skirt, but tonight she decided on an old pair of corded velvet slacks. She was in no mood tonight for Jim's exploratory love-making.

'What are we eating?' he asked, following her into the small kitchen.

'Cup-a-Soup, Welsh rarebit and coffee. OK?'

'Fine.'

His manner was decidedly restrained, and Lucille guessed she had hurt his feelings. 'Jim, I'm sorry,' she said impulsively. 'I didn't mean to snap at you back in the car.'

He laughed ruefully and gently touched her hair. 'That's all right. I'll get a couple of trays, shall I?'

'Yes, then go and put on one or two records.'

They had nearly finished their coffee when he stroked her hips and said, 'Why have you put those jeans on? I like your skirt best.'

'I know, but——'

He lifted up her chin and kissed her. 'Do you know what I'd planned for tonight?' She shook her head. 'I've got a bottle of champagne in the car. I was going to pop the question.'

She gave him a startled look. 'Pop the question? What question?' But she knew perfectly well what he meant.

'I was going to ask you to marry me, of course, you silly woman—or words to that effect. Not "Darling, be mine", or anything like that, but something on the lines of "How about you and me hitching up together", or "Two can live as cheaply as one" and all that.'

Lucille took a deep breath. She didn't want this.

Jim pointed a warning finger at her. 'Don't say "This is so sudden"!'

'Well, you have rather sprung it on me, haven't you?'

He shrugged. 'I don't know about that. Neither of us has been going out with anyone else for the past four or five months. I was under the impression that you liked me enough to—er—well, say yes to a proposition.'

She laughed briefly. 'And you were so confident that you brought along a bottle of champagne to celebrate!'

'Well, we could have drunk it, anyway. Still can. But you were so snappy on the way here, I began to get cold feet. Anyway, now that you know what I've got in mind, what about it?'

Lucille frowned and shook her head. 'I—I need time to think. There's this job I've been offered——'

'But what difference will that make? You can still carry on with your career if you want to. But what was this job you were offered—if I may ask without getting my head bitten off?'

She gave him an apologetic smile, then hesitated, knowing she would have to choose her words carefully, if she was to keep the identity of Mr Saunders secret as promised.

'It—it *is* a kind of secretarial job,' she told him. 'This man Gregory wants to buy up hotels abroad and he wants me to go with him, stay in them and write a report on the service and so on—just as an ordinary guest, incognito, as it were.'

Jim stared at her. 'How long for?' When she told him his eyes opened even wider. 'You're not going to take it, are you?'

'It's very tempting. A dress allowance, double my present salary and travel thrown in.'

'It sounds almost like bribery to me.'

'Bribery?' she queried.

'Yes, bribery—to get you away with him for six months.'

Lucille laughed, though he was only echoing her own vague suspicions. 'But that's ridiculous!'

'Is it? He certainly looked you over very well at the desk, didn't he?'

She took a deep breath. 'Why must you men always imagine that a woman is only offered a good job on a personal basis? It doesn't occur to you that I've got qualifications—such as the ability to speak several languages fluently and a smattering of a few more?'

'I'm well aware of that,' he rejoined. 'I'm also well aware of your many other qualifications. Your face, your figure, the oh-so-beautiful all of you.'

She shook her head. 'And so you think I'm being lured away to be sold on the white slave market?'

'Don't be silly! All I'm saying is, there's more to this than meets the eye. You don't even know the man.'

'He's a regular at the International—before our time. He told me so. You don't have to worry, he didn't take any great personal liking to me, nor I to him. Anyway, I've got until lunch time tomorrow to make up my mind.'

'It strikes me you've made it up already. And what about the question I've asked you? How long are you going to take to think about that?' Jim asked glumly.

Lucille looked at him for a moment. It was true that for the past four or five months they had seen each other most nights to the exclusion of any other friends. But marriage? It was something she had not even contemplated.

'I—I shall think about it, of course, Jim, but if I go on this job, can I let you know when I come back? I—have a feeling that I *will* go. The chance to travel, and be paid for the privilege, is too good an offer to pass up, simply because I don't happen to like the boss. I don't suppose I shall see much of him, anyway.'

'You sound as though you've already made up your mind,' Jim grumbled despondently.

'I shan't make it up definitely until tomorrow at one o'clock,' she told him.

'Lucille—don't go,' he said suddenly.

'But why not?'

He eyed her with exasperation. 'You're going away for six months with a man you hardly know—and you ask why not? Well, at least let's consider ourselves engaged before you go—if you *do* go.'

She shook her head. 'I can't do that. I told him I wasn't engaged and had no ties.'

'You did what?' he exclaimed.

'He wants six months' concentrated work with no distractions,' she told him. 'Now please, Jim, let's talk no more about it. It's my own decision. Six months will soon pass. I'll keep in touch, let you know where I am and all that, and—when I come back we'll talk about—well, about getting married, if you still feel that way.'

He gave her a long look. '*If I still feel that way.* You say the silliest things!'

He pulled her into his arms, and partly because she felt she had hurt him, she did not resist him.

When at last Lucille put out her bedroom light and settled down to sleep, she couldn't help thinking what a day and a half it had been. One's life went on normally day after day, doing the same things at the same time, then—wham! All at once one felt on the verge of great changes. In one day she had had two proposals, one of a new and exciting job, the other a proposal of marriage. She had to admit to herself that of the two offers, that of the job had by far the greatest appeal. She liked Jim, and who could tell, she might marry him one day, but right now, the idea of six months' travel was infinitely more tempting.

There was just one burning question. How would she get along with her boss?

The question haunted her throughout the morning as she stood behind the reception desk. Every now and then Jim darted her an enquiring look, but in the main she avoided conversation.

As the foyer clock moved ever nearer to one o'clock, however, he moved towards her.

'Have you decided, then, to take that job?'

Lucille shook her head impatiently. 'I—I don't know!'

'Well, you've got just about three minutes to make up your mind.'

'I know.'

'Then for goodness' sake, if there's any doubt in your mind at all, don't go,' Jim muttered urgently in her ear.

'May I have my key, please?' cut in an authoritative voice. Lucille swung round guiltily and Jim moved swiftly back to his own portion of the counter.

Lucille thought she might have known. It was Mr Saunders. He gave her a searching look from under his glowering dark brows, and she could guess what he was thinking. She reached up for his key with its heavy keeper, took it from its hook and laid it down on the counter with a defiant gesture. Of one thing she was certain: even if she accepted his offer she would not allow him to dictate to her about her friends—about her men friends in particular.

He picked up his key without a word and strode off in the direction of the lift.

'He didn't like that, did he, seeing you talking to me?' muttered Jim. 'What are you going to say to him? I thought you said nothing would ever induce you to work for a man like that?'

'It's not the man who interests me now, it's the job,' she answered.

'And the money?' he returned swiftly.

'Yes, why not? The money and the things it can buy—quite apart from the travel,' she flared back.

'Sorry,' he said contritely.

'That's all right,' she answered in a gentler tone. 'I know what's bugging you, but don't worry. I'll be back all in one piece, I assure you.'

'I expect you will, but I hate the thought of six months here without you, for one thing, and for another I somehow don't trust that man.'

'What you have to do is trust *me*,' she told him. 'Anyway, he looks a pretty cold fish, and don't forget I still haven't *quite* made up my mind.'

The hands of the clock were now definitely showing one o'clock. Lucille took her handbag from the cupboard and went to the staff room to tidy herself. All her natural instincts were to be punctual, yet she lingered, trying to feel sure about whether she would be doing the right thing in accepting this offer. But somehow there was an inevitability about it. She felt it in her bones that she would go, but at the same time she knew a strange reluctance, as if a small voice were trying to warn, trying to caution her. About what? She gave a small sigh and shook her head. She had better go upstairs; she was nearly five minutes late already.

In spite of that, she climbed the stairs rather than use the lift. She must not appear too eager at this second interview, she told herself. This morning she had replaced her grey suit of yesterday for one in white with a shirt in glowing apricot which set off her shining blonde hair. Whatever the outcome of the interview, she must look her best.

She tapped on Mr Saunders' door, and this time waited for him to open it, which he did. He gestured to her to enter, opening the door wide and giving her a top-to-toe scrutiny. She advanced into the room, feeling as though she were being examined like a museum piece.

'Do sit down,' came the voice behind her. 'You'll have a sherry?'

'Thank you.'

She seated herself in the same chair as before while he busied himself at the drinks table. He was formally dressed in a very fine suiting with a striped shirt and a tie which toned beautifully. Lucille wondered whether he had a wife who chose his clothes, and this set her thoughts on a track she had not considered before. Perhaps his wife would be coming with them on the trip—that was, providing she accepted the job and that he still wanted her.

He placed her drink on the small table beside her chair. 'I thought we might have lunch up here,' he said, 'then we can talk undisturbed for a little while.'

'Oh, well, I'm due back on Reception at two o'clock,' she told him. She had not expected this final interview to take more than a quarter of an hour at most.

'Don't worry about that,' he said authoritatively. 'I can soon get Ferrari to replace you.'

'Replace me?' echoed Lucille in a startled voice. He had decided to get rid of her whether or not she agreed to take the job he had offered?

'I mean, take your place for a little while, of course,' he amended, then added, 'If you decide to accept my offer, he will have to replace you, of course.'

'For six months,' she reminded him.

'Perhaps. Will you excuse me?'

He picked up the telephone and asked for luncheon menus to be sent up, leaving her wondering what on earth he had meant by the word 'perhaps'.

She waited for his explanation, but none came. He put down the telephone, poured himself a drink and sat opposite her. He looked at her, his glance flicking over her appearance again in a way she found most disconcerting. Perhaps she had been wrong to wear this outfit. The grey might have been more suitable, after all.

But greatly to her surprise he paid her a compliment. 'You're looking extremely smart this morning—just right for the kind of job I hope you'll accept.'

Pleased now that she had taken extra care with her appearance, Lucille noticed he had not asked her outright what her decision was. Perhaps he had already privately taken it for granted that it would be in the affirmative.

A waiter brought in the menus, and with a businessman's courtesy he consulted her, made suggestions and then ordered. Being more accustomed to Jim's more casual treatment, Lucille began to feel almost like royalty. Within a very short space of time the meal was brought up on a trolley, and with it a bottle of champagne in its ice bucket. She reflected that a man with Mr Saunders' kind of money could drink champagne any time he wanted to, not just on a special occasion like most people. She had noticed another thing too—he had not asked her whether she liked it. Not everyone did.

But as though reading her thoughts, he said, 'I trust you like champagne. Most women do.'

'I do, as a matter of fact,' she told him. 'In fact, I like most sparkling wines, they're so light. But I wouldn't assume that most other women do. I know quite a number who definitely don't like champagne.'

'Really? Don't you think that might be an affectation?'

'No. Why should it?'

He shrugged. 'A good champagne is considered fairly expensive, and different writers have given it a sort of glamour. A romantic association, if you like,' he said smoothly.

'Is that why you ordered it?' she answered without stopping to think.

She saw his dark brows raise a fraction. One of these days her tongue would land her in trouble!

'I used my judgement in your case, and obviously I was correct. You look the kind of woman who appreciates good things.'

He spoke in such a smooth, almost offhand manner, Lucille didn't know whether to feel complimented or not. He was a strange man, she decided. Not easy to understand at all. Perhaps he was still assessing her suitability for the job he was offering her. In fact, his next remark seemed to confirm this, in some respects.

'Apart from the sparkling wines and sherry, what other wines do you like? The still wines, I mean.'

'Chablis?'

He nodded. 'Very good. You prefer the white wines?'

'In general. The hocks, at any rate, are suitable with most dishes, although that might be largely a woman's choice. Many men like a mature red wine, especially with the meat course.'

The waiter informed them that 'luncheon was served', and Mr Saunders invited her to take her seat at the table-trolley. Lucille wondered how she could find out certain things about his tastes and so on without actually asking him directly. For example, what was his first name and whether he was married—or engaged—and whether his wife or girlfriend would be accompanying them on their trip.

After the main course had been served, he dismissed the waiter.

'We can help ourselves to the dessert,' he said, 'and I'll ring down when we're ready for coffee.'

While they were eating he asked Lucille about her family, what countries she had already visited and which countries she most wanted to see again, and her reasons. She was not quite sure whether he was taking it for granted that she was accepting his offer or not. He certainly did not ask her directly.

Then quite suddenly he said, in a changed voice, 'That young man you were talking to in Reception—is he a special friend of yours?'

'Well, I—I suppose he is, yes,' she answered, slightly taken aback.

'That's rather vague. Shall we be more specific? Has he asked you to marry him?'

Lucille drew an angry breath, but realised that he really was quite entitled to ask, even if not so bluntly.

'As a matter of fact, yes, he has.'

'I would have been surprised if he hadn't. And did you accept?'

'No, I did not.'

'Why not?'

'Because I was still thinking over your offer.'

'Was that the only reason?'

But Lucille decided this was one question too many. 'I decline to answer that, Mr Saunders. Sufficient to say that he and I are not engaged.'

'Ah! Does that mean you've decided to accept my offer?'

She hesitated. She wanted to say 'yes' right away, but an obstinate streak within her made her feel like keeping him guessing just a little while longer.

'Before I commit myself—tempting though your offer is—I'd like to know a few more details.'

'Such as?'

She asked the one question which, for some unknown reason, was uppermost in her mind.

'You said you wanted someone to travel with you. Would that include your wife?'

'No, it would not.'

'Why not?'

He flung down his serviette and crossed to the bell push. 'For the very simple reason that I have no wife,' he answered brusquely. 'Does it matter?'

'Not really.'

'Then why ask?'

'Curiosity, perhaps. Or maybe for the same reason that you wanted to be sure there would be no interference from a fiancé. I have a right to know, also, whether we shall be travelling alone or whether there would be a third person.'

'Whether we *shall* be?'

She had given herself away. But why not? She was nothing if not adventurous, and she had to answer him within the next few minutes. The fact that there was some antagonism between them would be a safeguard against any unwanted attention from him—although she couldn't see this man indulging in any idle flirtation. Then she amended her thoughts. Idle flirtation—no, but if she were any judge here was a man who knew what he wanted and would not take no for an answer.

The waiter came in with the coffee and took away the lunch things.

'Will you pour?' Mr Saunders asked Lucille. 'Then perhaps we can get down to business.'

'Certainly.'

Lucille became aware of a strange excitement. She was going to accept the job he was offering her, of course. She had known it all along. How could she do otherwise? She poured his coffee, which he took black with no sugar and then he seated himself opposite her as before.

'Now then, Miss LeFurve,' he said, in a businesslike voice. 'Let me have a straight answer from you. What have you decided?'

She closed her eyes momentarily and took a deep breath. Then, with a feeling as though she were jumping from the edge of a precipice, she told him, 'Yes, Mr Saunders. I—I accept your offer.'

CHAPTER TWO

BLAIR SAUNDERS rose to his feet. 'Good,' he said smoothly. 'Can you be ready in three days' time?'

'Three days!' Lucille echoed.

'Yes. I'd like to start out on Monday morning. The sooner the better, as I'm already behind schedule. We shall be travelling by car, of course, and I hope you're a good traveller—not liable to car-sickness or anything like that.'

He crossed to the writing table, leaving her speechless for a moment. Three days! She couldn't possibly be ready in so short a time, and she would tell him so too.

'Mr Saunders,' she began as he re-crossed the room to her, 'I'm afraid what you're asking is impossible.'

He gave her a haughty stare as if astonished at her temerity. 'Why is it impossible? You do have a valid passport, I hope?'

'Yes, but——'

'Here——' He thrust a cheque into her hands. 'I should think that will cover your needs for the moment.'

She looked at the cheque in astonishment. It was made out for two thousand pounds!

'But—but I can't possibly take this!' she exclaimed.

'Why not? I hope you're not going to question every item. You'll doubtless need to leave behind six months' rent for your flat. And I dare say you'll want to do a little shopping—though I shouldn't worry too much about extra clothes. There are plenty of shops where we're going. As to the rest of your arrangements, surely all you have to do is cancel the milk and the papers. I'll settle things here with Mr Ferrari.'

There seemed no more to be said. He had it all cut and dried. For two pins she would change her mind about the job. She wasn't accustomed to being hustled in this way. She rose to her feet and glanced down at the cheque in her hand.

'If you need any more, just let me know,' he told her. 'And don't worry about foreign currency—I'll take care of all that. Naturally, I shall pay all hotel bills and pay your salary as we go along.'

'I—I shan't need to spend all this before I—before we go,' Lucille said weakly, aware that she had confirmed her decision, rather than changed her mind. It really was dreadful, the effect this man had on her. She hadn't meant to say what she just had said at all.

'Then put the rest in your bank and take your cheque book with you,' he said patiently. 'You have a bank card?'

She nodded, feeling she had been cast in the role of the helpless female.

'Very well. And you're excused from further duty at the reception desk. I'll ring for Mr Ferrari right away. Be ready at six on Monday morning—I want to make an early start.'

His tone was plainly one of dismissal. In a daze Lucille crossed to the door, and almost without being aware of it found herself out in the corridor. She paused for a moment to collect her thoughts. Today was Friday; she had only two and a half days, not three. And as far as shopping was concerned only a day and a half. She glanced at her watch. In fact, she would only just have time to get the cheque she was holding into the bank and draw some money out before they closed.

Hurriedly she descended the stairs, and would have gone straight out had she not felt a hand on her arm.

'Lucy, for heaven's sake, where on earth are you going?'

She turned swiftly. 'Jim! Go back to Reception. You'll be in trouble if——'

'*I'll* be in trouble? *You're* supposed to relieve me for *my* lunch, remember?'

Lucille put her hand to her face. 'Oh, my goodness, yes, of course—I forgot! But I have to go out. I must get to the bank before it closes. I've been given the rest of the day off—in fact the weekend. Mr Ferrari will find somebody to relieve you.'

Jim stared at her. 'But why? What's happened, for goodness' sake?'

Lucille let out a distracted sigh. 'I can't explain now. Come round to my place when you've finished and I'll tell you all about it.'

She made her escape and was just in time to deposit the cheque in the bank and get some travellers' cheques. All of which left her with just over an hour before the shops closed and very little time to think of anything except what she would need for the journey and what from her wardrobe she could take with her. An extra lightweight case was a must, she decided, if she was going to buy clothes and other items during the six months she would be abroad.

She was going rather frantically through her wardrobe, rejecting this, pondering about that, when the doorbell of her flat rang. When she opened it to Jim she realised she had completely forgotten about him.

'Now what's all this about?' he demanded almost before he stepped over the threshold.

Lucille counted ten and forgave him, knowing how he felt. 'Have you eaten?' she asked.

'No,' he snapped.

'Well, neither have I. Come in, sit down and I'll go and rustle up something.'

He closed the door. 'I don't want to sit down. I want to know what happened up there this afternoon.'

'Then come into the kitchen and I'll tell you—but for heaven's sake calm down! You knew perfectly well there was a chance that I'd take this job I've been offered. Well, I have, and it starts on Monday morning—early. Now, what would you like, hamburgers or an omelette?'

'Never mind about the food. What I want to know is, why the rush? It seems to me you're ready to agree to anything this man suggests.'

Lucille froze for a moment and sent up a prayer for tolerance and patience.

'I am *not* willing to do quite everything either this man or any other suggests,' she said evenly. 'I decided to take the job, and the man who's employing me wants to set off for wherever is his first port of call on Monday morning, that's all.' She thought she'd better not mention the cheque or Jim would start talking about bribery— or worse.

'And where is his first "port of call", may I ask?' he returned in an interrogating tone of voice.

Lucille took a deep breath. 'I don't know. I'll send you a postcard the minute we check in at the first hotel.' He looked as though he might burst, and she thrust a tin in his hands. 'Here, open this—and don't say another word if you want us to part friends.'

'Part?' he echoed.

'Temporarily, I mean, of course,' she added hastily.

Lucille was glad when, at last, he had gone. It had been a full day, and a most ragged evening, especially as she had firmly said 'no' when Jim wanted to see her again over the weekend. He had protested vigorously, especially when it came to their usual Saturday night supper, but she shook her head.

'I'm sorry, really, Jim. But I'm going to need every minute between now and Monday morning. I shall be shopping tomorrow, then I'll have to wash my hair, and it will take me all of Sunday to pack. *And* I shall need an early night on Sunday.'

Reluctantly, he had left her, and when she returned to her task of looking through her wardrobe, she found a thrill of excitement beginning to stir inside her. A whole six months of travel! She could hardly believe her luck. Only one lingering element of doubt lurked in a corner of her mind. Would she find her boss too impossible to get along with? She hoped not, though his general attitude had been anything but cordial, and he was just the kind of man she liked least.

But as she put out her light and settled down to sleep, she told herself she did not have to like him, only do a good job, and that she was determined to do. Nothing would take away the pleasure she always felt when she was travelling to faraway places, when she was on the move.

Mr Saunders had arranged to call for her at her flat, and she was barely ready when he rang the bell.

'Ready?' he asked briefly, his glance taking in the easy-care two-piece outfit Lucille was wearing.

'In just a few minutes.'

'Are you packed?'

'Oh, yes, I've just got to——'

'I'll carry them down and wait for you downstairs,' he said in a clipped, businesslike voice.

In silence she showed him where her cases were, and he picked them up as if they were featherweight. Was he the kind of man who was naturally grouchy in the early morning, or was he making a special effort to ensure a boss-secretary relationship from the outset? Whatever it was, he was not the kind of man one kept waiting, she decided. She took a swift glance around to make sure everything was turned off that should be, touched up her face, then picked up her handbag and travel case, locked the door behind her and hurried downstairs, though as she reached the bottom step, she stopped hurrying and assumed a more dignified pace.

She had no intention of giving him the impression that she was afraid of him. The boss he might be, but she was not going to allow him to intimidate her.

He was just closing the boot of his car when she stepped out on to the pavement. As she might have expected, the car looked the last word in luxury, especially in comparison with Jim's more modest model in which they sometimes drove into the country.

'Shall I put that in the back seat for you?' asked Mr Saunders, taking her travel case from her.

She thanked him and went round to the passenger side. He was there before her and opened the door for her. She supposed this was the kind of courtesy habitual to a man in his position. But she couldn't help wondering about the women he must have in his life. Surely he had someone who would be reacting against his going off for six months with an employee? She could not believe that a man with all his advantages—and at this point in her musings she conceded that some women might find him attractive. He was good-looking, had plenty of money coupled with a certain something—a masculine attractiveness. She could not believe that somewhere there was not a special woman, or at least, someone who regarded him as special. A broken engagement? Or perhaps he was a born bachelor, a businessman so intent on making money that he never allowed himself to become attached to any one woman.

Almost without her being aware of it he had started the car and they were moving along. Lucille stole a glance at his strong profile. What kind of man was he underneath? Would she be able to get under his skin during the next six months, or would the period end as it had begun? She felt the remoteness of him, and surmised that he would not welcome conversation while he was driving. At any rate she would not attempt to talk unless he intimated that he wanted to.

'Are you comfortable?' he enquired after a little while.

'Oh, yes. It—it's a beautiful car.'

He nodded. 'It's one of the best, and it's well run in, so I'm not expecting any trouble. Do you drive?' he asked unexpectedly.

'Well—yes. I drove my mother's car at one time. But I haven't one of my own.'

'Did you enjoy driving?'

'To some extent, but parking is often something of a headache these days.'

'A chauffeur is the only answer,' he told her.

'If one can afford it, Mr Saunders. Few of us can,' Lucille answered tartly. Then she added in a milder tone, 'Anyway, living and working in London, it's hardly necessary to have one's own transport.'

He made no answer for a moment or two, then he said, 'If you agree, I think we might drop titles—they're rather cumbersome. My name is Blair. And yours, I believe, is Lucille.'

'Yes, that's right. And I agree, of course, although it will seem a little strange at first.'

'You'll get used to it. And it's the custom nowadays when two people are going to work closely together.'

So that established that. They were to be on first-name terms. Blair. Lucille said the name over to herself. It was an unusual one. Perhaps for that very reason it suited him. Because he was quite unlike any other man she had ever met. Her first reaction on seeing him enter the hotel had been one of dislike. But then she hadn't known he was the owner of the hotel. So what did she think of him now? she mused to herself. She was not quite sure, just as she was not sure what he thought about her. But, she told herself, they didn't have to like each other, only to be able to work together.

It was a strange experience, sitting in close proximity to a man she hardly knew and going she was not quite sure where. So far, he had told her little or nothing about their itinerary. As he had lapsed into silence again, she decided that the only way she was going to find out was by asking him.

So she did. 'Where are we heading?'

'Europe.'

Lucille knew a moment of irritation. How like a man to give you an inadequate answer so that you had to ask another question—or even a series of questions before you could get the right answer.

'Where—first—in Europe? Where shall we be to-night?' That should cover it.

'In Amsterdam, all being well. Have you been there?'

'Actually, no. I've tended to want to go farther afield— Italy, Greece, Turkey.'

'And Venice?'

'Yes, and Venice. I imagine Amsterdam is rather similar, except colder.'

Blair laughed briefly. 'The only similarity is that there's plenty of water.'

She bristled, feeling he was laughing at her. *'That,'* she said with emphasis, 'is precisely what I meant.'

She felt rather than saw him give her a swift, sidelong glance.

'That's not what you said. You implied that every-thing was similar except that it was colder. I'll grant you it's pretty cold in the winter. Otherwise, and apart from the canals, it couldn't be more different. Amsterdam is not, shall we say, as romantic a place as Venice. No gon-doliers serenading lovers along the Grand Canal. Amsterdam is a trading city.'

'Is that all?' Lucille returned pertly. 'No flowers, no art galleries, nothing like that?'

There was a moment's silence and again she feared her tongue had been too sharp. Not only sharp, but sar-castic too. Everyone knew of Holland's bulb industry, and the way the Dutch used flowers for decorative pur-poses. Holland was also famous for its art galleries, no-tably the Rijksmuseum. She was actually wondering whether she should apologise to him when he answered, 'Of course. But flowers are a business like anything else.'

A business—she might have known. Her half-formed idea of an apology died in her throat.

'And art? Is that a business too?' she challenged.

'That's for tourists—all a part of the business of tourism,' he answered.

For a moment she was at a loss for words. He was nothing less than a barbarian! she seethed. He saw everything in terms of money-making. Suddenly she hated herself for agreeing to work for such a man, for taking his money when, as yet, she had not earned it.

'Well?' he said, giving her a swift sidelong glance. 'Out with it. I can virtually see the sparks flying from you!'

His perceptiveness took her aback. 'Well, I—I was thinking, do you see everything in terms of business?' she asked, as he wanted to know what she was thinking.

'Most things, yes,' he answered. 'The world is kept going by businessmen. It's all a case of supply and demand.'

Supply and demand, Lucille's brain repeated. What a soulless way of looking at life! And she was going to have to endure this man's company for the next six months. She was beginning to think that by the time it was over she would have earned every penny of her generous salary and dress allowance.

'I suppose you care nothing at all for money,' Blair said suddenly in a sarcastic tone, adding, 'I've yet to meet a woman who doesn't.'

She drew an angry breath. 'There's all the difference in the world,' she retorted, 'between caring exclusively about it, and just caring enough to—to——'

'To buy you the luxuries as well as the needs?' he interposed.

'And what's wrong with that?' she demanded, stung by the truth of what he had said. She did like luxuries—when she could get them. She spent more money on clothes than she could really afford. She had far more expensive tastes than her salary would allow. All the same——

'There's nothing wrong with it,' he answered her. 'Just don't pretend that you don't care about money, that's all. It takes money to build art galleries, money to grow flowers, and none of it would be done without those businessmen you appear to despise. Money doesn't just drop from heaven, nor does it grow on trees.'

'I'm not saying it does,' Lucille retorted angrily. 'Why do you twist everything I say?'

They were at a traffic light. Blair turned slowly and looked at her, and she realised she had gone too far. He was, after all, her boss. She knew she had a temper, but she thought she had learned to control it in her job. She couldn't think what had come over her this morning.

'I—I'm sorry,' she blurted out.

He smiled slightly, put the car into gear, released the handbrake and moved forward again without speaking.

They reached Harwich in just over an hour and had breakfast in the restaurant of the ferry during the crossing. While they were eating Blair sketched over some of the things he wanted Lucille to look for when they were staying at the hotels he hoped to buy.

'I tell you this,' he said in a tone she had not heard him use before, and jabbing a forefinger in her direction. 'By the time we've finished you'll probably have had enough travelling to last you for a lifetime. You'll certainly have earned the salary I'm paying you. Remember, you're not on holiday.'

'I'm aware of that—*Mr Saunders*,' she flashed back. If he was going to start using bullying tactics, she thought, she certainly was not going to call him Blair!

But he was having none of that. 'I told you to call me Blair. At some of the hotels we stay in we shall act like strangers, at others it may be necessary for us to share a suite.'

Lucille drew in her breath swiftly. '*What?* Oh, no, Mr Blair Saunders. Anything like that is definitely out!' She got to her feet, but he grasped her wrist swiftly across the narrow table.

'And where do you think you'd go? Swim back to shore? I tell you it may be necessary. I want a sample of every kind of accommodation each hotel has to offer.' He gave her a penetrating look. 'Don't worry, I shan't try to seduce you. I'm on a business trip.'

Now, for some reason, she felt she had received a slap in the face. She had thought he might be a reasonable man to work for, but now she was beginning to wonder. He was certainly making sure that their boss-employee relationship was firmly established. She felt annoyed that it was he who had done so. She felt it should have been the other way round, and she was confused by a deep-down sensation of disappointment. She dismissed the feeling and lifted her chin.

'Thank you for your reassurance—*Blair*, but let me tell you, you would have a great deal of difficulty in succeeding, even if you tried.'

His dark brows raised slowly and an odd glint came into his eyes as he looked at her across the table. Lucille's heart gave a small leap. He looked almost as though he would try there and then.

Then he said in a voice like cold steel, 'Let's get back to business, shall we? I trust you've brought a nice big notebook with you?'

'Of course.'

'Good. Each hotel must, of course, be judged on its price and surroundings, its location. There are, however, a number of things which should be carefully noted as routine. The plumbing, for instance. General cleanliness, the service at meals, the state of the interiors. The exteriors you can leave to me. What, by the way, is the first thing you look for in a hotel?'

Lucille breathed an inward sigh of relief that they were on a less explosive topic.

'After a courteous reception—and whether or not one is shown to one's room or has one's own luggage to carry up, I think the bed is what most people consider important, including myself. The mattress should be neither too hard nor too soft—most hotels err on the soft side, because they're slow to make replacements—and the other thing is the pillows. The same, or similar, should apply. Neither too full nor too much the other way—and feather, of course. So many hotels are penny-pinching, and I shouldn't think it really pays in the end.'

Blair nodded, but still he had a quibble. 'And what about cleanliness? Isn't that important too?'

'Of course. That goes without saying,' she answered.

'Nothing goes without saying,' he said sharply.

Lucille gritted her teeth, but she simply had to answer him. 'You did ask me what I considered to be the most *important* things,' she pointed out. 'One has to choose, and providing the rooms are not actually filthy, I consider sleeping comfort to be pretty essential. The first thing most people do when they get into their hotel bedroom is to test the mattress.'

'I'll take your word for it,' he said grudgingly. 'But I want you to report on everything in every hotel where we stay. Beds, service, food, the number of times the linen is changed—everything. In the main you'll have rooms with a bath. I'll sample the others and talk to the staff. Your job will be to mingle with the other guests. They will be people of all nationalities, not just English tourists, and that's where your command of languages will come in useful.'

'I see. But if you want to talk to the staff—what about your own language ability?'

'Oh, don't concern yourself on my account. I have enough of a smattering of most languages to get by on. What I want to do is devise ways and means of getting into the kitchens. If they knew who I was, of course, I'd have no trouble, but I want to see things as they really are—now, before I decide to buy.'

He was all businessman. Lucille couldn't help wondering why he had insisted on first names at all. She had had to bite back several times an inclination to call him 'sir'. He had certainly not used her first name yet. He was a strange man, she decided. But it would suit her just fine if they kept on a businesslike basis.

They arrived in Amsterdam just in time for lunch, and Lucille thought it all quite fantastic, as Blair drove alongside canals and over bridges to their hotel, which overlooked one of the main canals, not far from Dam Square. Blair had been quite right, really, she had to admit to herself as she looked eagerly this way and that. Apart from the water—wet wherever you went!—there was no comparison in the architecture with Venice. The two were entirely different. She had known this, of course, having seen photographs, but photographs never make the same impression. She found it extraordinary and quite fascinating the way the tall, narrow houses nudged each other for space, giving the impression of fighting for elbow room in order to have a view of the water. Lucille craned her neck to admire the high gables, each one different. Some were shaped like a bell, others were more triangular or went up in kind of steps, while one or two were suggestive of an ornate fireplace or cornice. But she liked the bell-shaped ones best.

'You'll get a crick in your neck,' Blair warned her as her gaze was held by the heavy wooden hoists which protruded a few feet out from each gable. She had read about this method of getting items of furniture into the houses, but it was fascinating to see them.

'I'd love to see someone trying to hoist a piano up or something like that,' she said.

'I'm sure you would,' he said with heavy sarcasm. 'But I'm equally sure it's a positive nightmare to anyone responsible.'

A porter appeared from the hotel to take their bags. 'Full marks for service, anyway,' Lucille murmured as her bags were lifted out of the car.

'Don't be in too big a hurry to award marks,' Blair told her. 'Wait until you see what the service is like at mealtimes and so on.'

Lucille gave an inward sigh. He was going to be quite difficult to please, this boss of hers. But he did carry his own luggage into the hotel, she noticed, leaving the porter to carry hers.

She couldn't help smiling to herself as a sudden thought occurred to her. She would devise a system of star ratings for service, food, etc., and at the same time she might record a credit and debit account for her boss. At times he was insufferable, at others he showed a different side of himself. It would be interesting to see how he averaged.

Blair put down his cases and approached the reception desk. Lucille followed, standing just a little behind him.

'Name, sir?' enquired the receptionist.

'Saunders. Blair Saunders from Britain.'

'Ah.' The young man's eyes flicked to Lucille. 'Mr and Mrs Saunders.'

Lucille's eyes widened. What an appalling mistake for a receptionist to make! One should never assume that because a man and woman arrived at a hotel together they were husband and wife. It could be amusing, in a way, but—— She wished she could see Blair Saunders' face. But there was no need. His voice, severe and clipped, was enough.

'The young lady's name is Miss Lucille LeFurve, and two separate rooms are booked,' he said.

'Oh! Oh, I beg your pardon, sir,' said the receptionist in some confusion, though he recovered swiftly as he found their names in his book. 'Yes, that's right. Adjoining rooms—all right?' He beamed from one to the other.

Lucille was about to protest and say that it was not 'all right', but to her surprise Blair nodded, and the next moment the receptionist handed two sets of keys to the porter and they proceeded to the lift. Lucille relaxed. Obviously the word adjoining simply meant that the rooms were next door. When they reached the fourth floor, her luggage was taken into room number 400, while Blair opened the door to 401. When she looked around the room, however, she did discover a door which certainly did not lead to the bathroom. She turned the knob gingerly, but it would not open either way. Neither was there any sign of a key anywhere. It was clear, she thought, that the communicating doors were only used when guests wanted them, or perhaps nowadays they were never used.

She went over to the window and looked out on to the busy scene below: boats of all shapes and sizes, houseboats, cars parked on the quayside, people on bicycles. If her boss did not want her this afternoon, she would love to explore a little.

She heard a knock and turned to see the knob of the communicating door turning slowly, just as she herself had turned it. She gave a mischievous smile and decided to play a little joke on him.

'Come in,' she called out, certain that if there was no key on this side there would not be on that either.

She almost burst out laughing when the knob turned again and the door wouldn't open. She went towards it and called out, 'I'm afraid it's locked!'

She couldn't hear the answer Blair gave, but after a few minutes there came a knock on the other door. She opened it and Blair stood there.

'It's lunch time,' he informed her with a hard stare. 'Are you ready to come down?'

'Will you—give me a minute to wash my hands and tidy up? I'm afraid I've been gazing through the window. Perhaps you'd like to come in for a few minutes.'

Quickly Lucille washed her hands and tidied her hair in the small bathroom. When she emerged he too was looking down at the canal scene.

'Does your room have a view of the water?' she asked him.

'No, that's a privilege I accorded to you. All houses and hotels in Amsterdam are long and narrow, so only a minimum number can have a room with a view. But of course, we want to sample all kinds of rooms for our purpose. I shall be making my own notes, naturally.'

'Yes, of course.'

Lucille had to keep telling herself that she was not here on holiday, that the man sitting opposite her at lunch was her employer. For a brief moment she wished it were not so, but quickly dismissed the thought. It was going to be as much as they could do to get along on a business footing.

'You were saying earlier,' he broke into her thoughts, 'that a hotel bed was of prime importance, in your opinion. Have you tried yours yet?'

She shook her head. 'I haven't really had time.'

'You've had time to gaze out of the window. That seems to suggest that you rate the view as being more important than a sagging mattress.'

She wished she dared kick his shins under the table. 'It doesn't suggest anything of the kind,' she answered, somewhat staggered at her rashness. But she rushed on, 'To begin with, not every hotel has a view worth looking at. I still say that the majority of people bounce on the bed first. In any case, if one had to choose between the two—a room with a view or a comfortable bed, naturally it would be the bed.'

Blair eyed her in silence for a long moment—so long, in fact, that another apology was on the tip of her tongue. Wretched man! she thought to herself. Why does he goad me so much, and why should I keep having to apologise?

'I'm glad you think so,' he said tersely. 'And may I suggest that you keep it that way.'

At this undoubted ticking off, Lucille almost answered, 'Yes, sir.' But she managed to bite her tongue. After all, he was the boss. Why couldn't she just accept the fact? She could not answer her own question.

'Do you want to rest this afternoon?' he asked. 'After all, it's been quite a long journey.'

She shook her head. 'Time is too precious. I'd like to explore a little, if I may.'

'Certainly. We'll go right after lunch.'

She opened her mouth to say she would prefer to go alone, but once more thought better of it and reminded herself again that she was not here on holiday. It really was going to be difficult to keep remembering this.

They went out on foot, and a sense of pleasure settled on her. It was quite obvious that Blair knew his way around, and Lucille was enchanted as they crossed the many bridges and surveyed the scene all around them. Everywhere, the houses were packed together, so different from the detached and semi-detached nature of English houses, the wide-fronted shops. And yet the Dutch had not resorted to building skyscrapers.

'I'm all for our hotels having guide books and street maps on sale—and maps of the surrounding districts,' Lucille remarked as they retraced their steps back to the hotel.

'*Our* hotels?' queried Blair.

'Well then—*your* hotels,' she amended.

'No, no,' he answered swiftly. 'Our hotels will do.'

She took a swift glance at his face, but could read nothing from his expression. If only she knew, sometimes, what was going through his mind!

To her intense disappointment Blair was not in to dinner. A note was handed to her by the head waiter as she sat down to eat, having waited in vain for him to knock on her door as he had at lunchtime.

'Please excuse me,' the note said. *'I'm dining with an old friend.'*

Lucille was astonished at the pang of disappointment she felt. An old friend, she repeated to herself. It would be a woman, of course. A man of Blair Saunders' means and personality would have women friends all over the place, she thought, somewhat peevishly.

She was half-way through her silent meal and wishing she was back in London when she noticed a man looking in her direction. He was sitting at a table alone. Lucille looked away again, but each time she glanced in his direction she found he was still looking at her. She had half a mind to encourage him, just to see what Blair's reaction would be if he returned and found her with someone, but the man was probably a native of Holland, and as she could not speak Dutch, conversation would be impossible.

However, she had reached the coffee stage of her meal when the waiter handed her a note, and indicated that it came from the other guest. The note read: *'Please may I join you for coffee?'* The signature, as far as she could make out, was Timothy Collins. It sounded English. She scribbled the word 'yes' underneath and gave it back to the waiter. In a very short space of time Mr Collins was at her table holding out his hand to her.

'Good evening. Timothy Collins is the name—in case you couldn't read my writing.'

'Ah, you're English. My name's Lucille LeFurve. Do sit down,' she said, shaking his hand.

'LeFurve?' he queried with a smile. 'Are you French? If so, you haven't a trace of accent.'

Lucille shook her head. 'I was born in the Channel Islands, but have lived in London for most of my life.'

'Are you on holiday?' he asked.

She explained. 'And you?'

'I'm here on business too. Diamonds—industrial diamonds. I'm glad you're English, I had to take a chance. How long will you be in Amsterdam?'

'I'm not sure. It's up to my boss,' said Lucille.

'Perhaps I'll be able to see more of you?'

But of that she could not be sure. He was a good-looking man—light brown hair, in his forties, she imagined. 'I'm sorry,' she told him, 'but I'm afraid I don't feel free to make any arrangements.'

'But you're free this evening? Perhaps we could go for a walk or maybe go into one of the brown cafés.'

'Brown cafés?' she queried.

'The nearest thing to an English pub. They probably get their name from the colour of the décor. The name is supposed to have been coined by an Amsterdam journalist.'

Lucille accepted the invitation. After all, she had been left to her own devices. Why shouldn't she go out?

The city was ablaze with light and colour. Naturally, with so many canals, the lights of the houses, restaurants and other buildings were reflected brilliantly in the black water like a veritable fairyland. It was beautiful, and could, Lucille thought regretfully, have been very romantic. But one could hardly be romantic with a man one had only just met. She found herself thinking of Blair Saunders again. How romantic would he be? she wondered.

A few minutes later she thought her imagination was playing her tricks. She saw him walking into what her companion told her was the most expensive hotel in

Amsterdam, and clinging on to his arm was the most beautiful woman Lucille had ever seen.

'I might have known,' she muttered more to herself than to Timothy.

'What?' he asked.

'That beautiful woman over there in the white dress with the—the distinguished-looking man.'

His gaze followed hers. 'Must be made of money, going in there. Even I would think twice, and I'm not poor.'

'That's my boss,' she said in a flat tone of voice.

'And the woman?'

'I've never seen her before.'

Timothy looked at her face. 'It doesn't really matter to you, does it? I mean——'

Lucille shook her head. 'Heavens, no!' she said emphatically. 'Let's go and find one of those brown cafés you were telling me about. They sound more to my taste than the place they've gone into.'

'Good.'

But she found she did not altogether care for the one he took her to—and he assured her they were all much the same. It was noisy and crowded and there was barely standing room, still less sitting room. After a glass of what was called *pilsjes*, Lucille said she would like to go back to their hotel.

'But it's early yet,' Timothy protested.

'I know, but actually I have some work to do.'

'Work? At this hour?'

'Well, yes. Some records I have to keep. If I don't write things down while they're fresh in my mind, I'm likely to forget.'

There was no light coming from Blair's room as she passed it on the way to her own. With a girl like that, he would almost certainly be out late, she thought, as she turned the key in her lock sharply.

She sat up in bed and made a few notes on the service and general facilities of the hotel, after which she read for a short while, then finding her eyes beginning to sting, she put out her light and closed them.

Whether she had fallen asleep she was not quite sure, but she was aroused by a clicking noise. The light was shining under the communicating door. Then came the sound of the knob being turned, and very slowly the door opened and Blair Saunders stood framed there in his dressing-gown.

CHAPTER THREE

LUCILLE stared silently without moving. What did he want? What was the time? Where had he found a key to the door?

She waited for him to close it again, but instead of that he approached the bed. She drew in her breath sharply and reached out for the switch on her bedside lamp. As the room flooded with light, she drew the sheet up to her neck.

'What are you doing here?' she demanded in a pitch higher than she normally spoke in. 'Get out of my room immediately! You had no right to come in here at all!'

Blair's eyes widened and he folded his arms in the manner of having no intention of doing any such thing. The next moment he was sitting at the bottom of her bed. Lucille slid down swiftly, her eyes darting to her dressing-gown on the back of a chair. But she would have to get out of bed in her nightdress to reach it.

He saw her dilemma and gave a grim smile. 'Don't worry,' he told her, 'you're quite safe.'

The way he said it was almost insulting. 'I sincerely hope I am safe, as you put it,' she answered tartly. 'All the same, I would still like you to go—and leave the key to that door with me. Where did you get it, may I ask?'

'You may ask, but I don't have to tell you. And now I'd like to ask *you* something. Where have you been— and with whom? I came in an hour ago and was told you'd gone out with one of the guests—a man, of course.'

'So?' Lucille drew her dignity around her as well as the sheet. 'Why do you say "of course" in that tone of voice? Is my every move to be questioned? Surely I'm entitled to *some* free time?'

He stood up, a peculiar glint in his eyes as he looked down at her, and Lucille clutched the sheet even more tightly. With that look in his eyes there was no telling what he had in mind. If he tried anything what should she do? Scream? But there might be no one to hear her.

'Please remember,' he said, 'that you're in a foreign country whose language you don't understand—in this instance. As I'm responsible for your being here and you're in my employ, I have a certain responsibility for you. I left you a note telling you I was going out: I expect the same courtesy from you. While we're on this project, I want as far as possible to know your whereabouts. Is that understood?'

'Well—yes, I suppose so,' she answered, seeing the sense in what he said. All the same——

'Good,' he said before she could say anything else, and turned and walked off, leaving her fuming. Why did he always somehow manage to have the last word?

He closed the communicating door behind him and she heard the key turn in the lock before she realised that he still had the key, the only one as far as she knew. That meant he could just come and go as he pleased. She jumped out of bed and snatched up her dressing gown. Crossing swiftly to the communicating door, she banged on it loudly.

'Mr Saunders! Give me that key,' she called out. 'I demand to have it!'

There was no reply. The next moment the chink of light showing under the door vanished. For a moment she hesitated, her hands clenched angrily. He couldn't do this to her. He had no right, and she was not going to let him get away with it. She banged on the door again, this time with both fists. Still there was no response, and she suddenly realised that she was hurting her hands. She ceased her knocking and rubbed them. Infuriating man! What was she to do? She sat on the bed for a moment or two glaring at the communicating door. In the morning she would speak to the manager and insist that Mr Blair Saunders surrendered his key, but for the present there was little she could do but get into bed and try to sleep. She did not suppose for a moment he would come into her room again tonight.

As a precaution, however, and so that she would certainly hear him if he tried, she wedged a chair under the knob of the door. In future she would refuse to occupy a room which had a communicating door.

Lucille slept fitfully that night, and as a consequence slept late. She had intended to do some work on her reports before going down to breakfast, but as it was, she had to make a very hurried toilet before going downstairs. Blair had nearly finished his breakfast.

'Good morning,' he said, giving her a keen glance. 'I was just wondering what was keeping you. Did you oversleep?'

'Thanks to you,' she answered boldly, 'I couldn't get to sleep for ages last night, and when I did I kept waking up and having bad dreams. Then I slept when I should have been waking up.'

'And have come down to breakfast in a bad temper,' he said coolly.

'I am *not* in a bad temper!' she flared.

'No? Well, have some coffee. It'll make you feel better.'

He poured some out for her, then gestured to a waiter to bring a fresh pot. Lucille murmured her thanks, still feeling annoyed with him, and took the cup of coffee. It was then that Blair noticed how bruised her hands were, and enquired how they had come about.

'I hurt them banging on that door last night,' she told him pointedly.

His brows shot up. 'So it was you? I wondered what the noise was.'

'You knew perfectly well who it was,' she answered accusingly.

'Did I? And why, then, were you making such a noise?'

'I wanted that key. I have no intention of——' She was halted by the steely glint which had come into his eyes and the tightening of his jaw, and reminded herself once again that he was her boss.

'Get on with your breakfast, please, Lucille. We have work to do. And don't worry about the key—I've handed it in at Reception. I found it in one of my drawers. Let that be an end of the matter,' said Blair in a tone of voice which put her unquestionably in her place.

Lucille made a selection of the various breakfast dishes offered her and ate without tasting anything. She was beginning to wish she had never come on this job. He was proving to be a most exacting and difficult man to get along with. And she somehow hated this feeling that she must always be biting her tongue, remembering that he was her employer. At the same time she realised that she ought really to treat him with more respect. But it was difficult somehow, she argued with herself. He did not always behave like an employer. Travelling together like this and having meals at the same table, it was not easy to maintain the correct boss-secretary relationship. All the same, she told herself, she must try.

'How long are we staying here?' she asked.

'Just one more night, that's all. I shall be in to dinner tonight,' he added. 'And I'd like you to join me.'

'Very well,' she answered, knowing that behind the mild request lay an order.

'What was the food and the service like yesterday evening?' he asked. 'I presume you did eat at the hotel?'

'Of course. And it was an excellent meal, well served and beautifully cooked. No faults to find at all.'

'And how did it come about that you became acquainted with this—man you went out with?'

It was on the tip of her tongue to say that was a private matter and nothing to do with her job as his secretary, but she thought better of it, and gave him a brief account of how Timothy Collins had approached her and where they had been.

'As it happens, he was English,' she told him.

'And have you made any other arrangements to go out with him?' She shook her head. 'Good, then perhaps you'll accompany me on a night tour of the city.'

'Delighted.' Then she added with a hint of mischief: 'Not seeing your "old friend", then?'

He gave her an odd look across the table. 'No,' he answered briefly.

And with that she had to be content. A few minutes later he left her to finish her breakfast alone, saying he would see her at lunch.

Lucille felt strangely disappointed. She had expected that they would spend the whole day together. Blair had not even told her whether he wanted her to do anything in particular.

She felt a hand on her shoulder and a voice bade her 'good morning'. She looked up to see Timothy Collins.

'How are you this morning?' he asked her.

'Fine. And you?'

He nodded. 'Can you have lunch with me today?'

She shook her head. 'Sorry—a lunch date with the boss.'

At that moment Blair suddenly appeared again. 'I do hope I'm not interrupting anything,' he said with heavy sarcasm.

Lucille made a swift introduction. Blair eyed the other man suspiciously and gave him a cool nod, then said to him, 'Do you mind if I have a few words in private with my—with Miss LeFurve?'

Timothy murmured that he would 'see her around' and made off to his own table for a late breakfast.

Lucille glanced at Blair's dark face. 'Is anything the matter?'

He darted a look at Timothy's back, then to Lucille. 'Who is he?' he demanded.

'He's a diamond merchant. And he's the man with whom I went out last night,' she told him.

'I see. Are you always so quick in forming new acquaintanceships?'

She gave him a hard stare. 'I make friends easily—yes, if that's what you mean. Perhaps you and I should get a few things clear, Mr Saunders.'

He returned her stare with a steely look of his own. 'I don't know what you have in mind, but I made everything perfectly clear to you before we embarked on this project. I want six months' concentrated work with no distractions. I came back to tell you that we're moving on tomorrow morning, and what I'd like you to do between now and lunch time is take a look at some of the shops, note what kind of things they sell and assess prices and values. And here——' he dropped a wad of Dutch notes on the table, 'buy yourself something. Make believe that you're a tourist. Will that suffice?'

Lucille looked at him blankly for a moment. 'I—I should think so, but——'

'No buts,' he cut in brusquely. 'I'll see you at lunch, and in case I forget to mention it later, I'll see you in the hotel lounge at seven o'clock sharp this evening.'

As he stalked off, Lucille began to recover herself, and her anger rose. She reached out for the sugar bowl and would have dearly loved to throw it at his retreating back. When he had been interviewing her in London, he had been fairly reasonable. Now he was showing himself in his true colours. He was proving to be the driving, unreasonable, twenty-four-hour boss. She hated him! For two pins she would catch the first plane back to London. She gathered up her things, including the Dutch currency, and walked angrily to the lift and went up to her room. By the time she reached it, however, her anger was evaporating. Blair was paying her well—she had to admit that. And there was more travel to come. What did it matter that they did not like each other? Perhaps it was just as well. She was here on a job of work, anyway.

Noting, for the sake of her report, that her bed had already been made and clean towels put out, Lucille put a small notebook in her handbag and went out. She had not planned to go looking at the shops this morning; she had wanted to look at the old part of the city and perhaps go down to the harbour. Was this going to be the general pattern? Blair would not tell her how long they were staying in one place, nor give her much opportunity to plan her own free time. Her lips firmed into a determined line. She would just have to have it out with him. As it was, he was going to commandeer both the afternoon and the evening.

The shops were interesting, of course, but in the main they stocked the same kind of things that any major city did: clothes, furniture, food, jewellery, and—her attention was held—Delft pottery. It would have been fascinating to have visited the factory, which she understood was not far out of Amsterdam. But Blair had not mentioned such an excursion. She was beginning to realise the difference between foreign travel on a job of work and that of being on holiday when one could please oneself which places to visit. But, she told herself, she could always return some other time, and with her generous salary she would be able to save some money for that purpose.

The thought of money reminded her of the currency Blair had given her that morning. It was quite a considerable amount. Had he intended to make it a part of her salary? Not as a gift, surely? She certainly couldn't accept the latter, and if it was to be part of her salary, she was not prepared to spend too much.

In a narrow street off Dam Square, Lucille spent some time looking at the many different kinds—and prices—of Delft pottery. She knew, of course, that a good deal of what was sold in shops like these was merely imitation of that made in the seventeenth century, but it was attractive, all the same. There were some finely shaped pieces, carefully painted in imitation Chinese blue and white porcelain and lacquerwork. There were also figures in imitation of Meissen porcelain, and it was difficult to choose. She thought of Jim and bought him a kingfisher perched on a bare branch, and for herself a beautifully designed vase and a decorative plate which almost matched. She wondered if she should buy something for Blair, and after a great deal of hesitation chose a squat vase in imitation porcelain. If he didn't like it or showed any sign of being put out by the gift she could give it to someone else—or keep it for herself.

She dropped her purchases in the straw bag she was carrying, and going out of the door almost collided with Blair Saunders himself.

She gave a gasp of surprise. But he did not look in the least surprised.

'I thought I might find you here,' he said.

Lucille eyed him suspiciously. Was he checking up on her? 'Did you want me for anything in particular?' she asked.

'Yes and no,' he answered cryptically. 'Have you bought anything in here?'

'Three items, actually.'

'Three—rather than one good one? Are they all for yourself?'

She wondered why all the questioning. 'They're not all for myself—no,' she answered. 'Two are—presents. I can pay for those out of my own money. All of them, in fact,' she added.

'Oh, for goodness' sake!' he snapped with some annoyance. 'Come and have a coffee.'

He grasped her arm so hard she could have cried out. She wondered if something had happened to annoy him—perhaps something to do with the woman he had been with the previous evening.

'Show me what you've bought,' he commanded when they had been served with their coffee.

Wondering how much more of his—bullying almost—she could take, Lucille obediently unwrapped her purchases and showed them to him.

'I thought you said you'd only bought three items?' he queried as she placed them all on the table.

'These two,' she explained, pointing to the vase and plate, 'are for myself. I thought they'd look nice in my flat. And I'm paying for those myself,' she added swiftly.

Blair appeared to ignore her last remark. Picking up the two items she had indicated, he examined them thoroughly. 'Mm. Not bad,' he pronounced. 'You have good taste.'

'Thank you,' she answered, although he had somehow managed to make it sound more like a statement than a compliment.

'And the other two?' he queried. 'Who are they intended for?'

'Er—this is for a friend of mine who works in your London hotel,' she said, picking up the kingfisher.

'Ah, yes—the young man in Reception. Obviously you know his taste, so I won't comment. And this?' he asked, holding up the vase she had chosen for him.

Lucille hesitated, beginning to regret her impulse. He had not exactly been complimentary about the kingfisher. However, she gathered together her courage.

'I bought that for you.'

His eyes widened. He gave her a long look and murmured something she could not quite catch. Then he said again, 'Mm. Well now, let me see.'

She almost felt as if she were on trial. She practically held her breath as he examined the vase. It was a representation of the Chinese porcelain of the K'ang period which could probably be used as either a tobacco jar or equally well as a biscuit barrel, as it had a lid. Or even as just an ornament. But perhaps he did not like ornaments.

'Yes, very nice,' he said at last. 'But why buy me a gift? That isn't what I gave you the money for.'

'I understood that it was given to me to spend as I wished, to make believe I was a tourist,' she answered.

'I said "buy your*self* something",' he corrected.

'And so I have,' she argued. Then, as a look of impatience crossed his face, 'Don't you want the vase?'

'Of course—now that you've bought it.'

'I'll pay you back for—for Jim's present,' she told him, suddenly realising that she had, in effect, bought a present for Jim out of her employer's money.

'Oh, for heaven's sake stop quibbling about the money!' snapped Blair. 'But another time, if I give you money to spend on yourself, do so.'

Lucille bit her lip. She felt like a child who had been chastised. She wanted to snap back at him, to retort that she would never take money from him again except her rightful salary, but she conceded to herself that he had a valid point, so she held her tongue and began to wrap up the articles again and put them into her bag. There was a long silence. Lucille stole a swift glance at his face and was surprised to see how tense his jaw was and how dark his expression. She was wondering what she should say to him—whether to apologise once more—when he pushed back his chair.

'Let's go. I have some papers to read, and I dare say you have some work to do too.'

'Yes, of course.'

She gathered up her things and they walked back to the hotel almost without speaking. Lucille had the distinct feeling that Blair was annoyed about something. She had fully expected to be able to spend the entire morning looking around the shops. As it was, it was only just after eleven. She was finding it very difficult to keep up with his changes of mood.

As they entered the hotel Timothy Collins was sitting in the foyer. He rose immediately and walked towards them.

With a brief nod to Blair, he said to Lucille, 'Can I speak to you for a moment?'

'Yes, of course.' Lucille turned to her employer, but before she could speak he had turned without a word and was walking rapidly towards the lift. Lucille looked after him and sighed.

'Trouble?' queried Timothy.

She shook her head. 'Not really, but I'd better not linger, if you don't mind. As you know, I'm not really here on holiday.'

Timothy led her to a seat. 'I realise that, but surely you're not expected to keep strict office hours, and if you are, what about coming out with me this evening? I have to leave Amsterdam first thing in the morning.'

'We're moving on too. I'm sorry—really.'

'Perhaps we can keep in touch. I'd like to see you again, that is, if you——'

She shook her head, thinking of Jim. 'I'm not sure what my plans will be in the future,' she explained.

Timothy gave a rueful smile. 'Come to that, which of us is? But what about tonight?'

'I'm sorry, truly, but I'm doing a night tour of the city with Mr Saunders.'

'And this afternoon?'

'That too is all arranged, I'm afraid.'

'My goodness, he's keeping a tight rein on you, isn't he?'

'At the moment, yes.' Lucille rose and held out her hand. 'Goodbye, Timothy. Perhaps we shall meet again one day, who knows? But I must go now.'

Timothy rose too, and took her hand in both his own.
'I shall find you, never fear.' He leaned over and kissed
her, and at that moment the lift door opened and Blair
stepped out. Guiltily, Lucille withdrew her hand from
Timothy's and said a quick goodbye before turning and
almost colliding with Blair.

'Where are you going?' he demanded.

She bristled at his tone. 'To my room,' she answered
with barely concealed anger. 'Do you mind?'

He gave her a barbed look. 'I trust you haven't made
any arrangements to see that man again?'

Lucille did not answer him. She swept past him to the
lift and made her way to her room. Was he going to be
like this for the rest of their time abroad—six months?
she wondered as she dropped her purchases on to her
bed. If so, life was going to be pretty intolerable, and
she was not sure she could put up with it—not for all
the money in the world. She simply could not think what
she had done to annoy him so.

She crossed to the window and fumed for a while,
wondering whether to tackle him about his attitude, or
simply to tell him she was going back to London.

Automatically she picked up the wallet containing her
notes and her report, so far, on the hotel in which they
were now staying. It was interesting work. Blair was also
paying her well, she had to admit that. And there was
a lot more travel—which she loved—to come. What if
she did return to London? The hotel manager would by
now have had her replaced as receptionist.

She sighed. She had better calm down. What did it
matter if she and her boss did dislike each other? Perhaps
it was just as well, and she would simply have to learn
to put up with his moods.

She left her room and went downstairs to the hotel
lounge, which overlooked the canal. She ordered a soft
drink and as tactfully as she could had a conversation
with the barman about the pay and conditions of the

staff and, accompanied by a generous tip, extracted as much information as she could think of. On one thing she was determined: she was not going to give Blair Saunders any reason to find fault with her work.

Before going in to lunch she slipped upstairs to her room to deposit her wallet and to tidy up. When she reached their table, Blair was waiting for her.

'And what have you been doing with yourself since I saw you down in the foyer talking to Mr Collins?' he asked almost before she was seated.

Lucille offered up a silent prayer for patience. 'I've been working,' she told him.

His brows raised a fraction. 'Really?'

'What do you think I've been doing?' she countered, stung by the scepticism in his tone. 'Look, Mr Saunders,' she continued, 'I'm quite well aware that I'm not here on holiday—as you reminded me earlier. Would you like to see my notes now—I can go and get them this minute—or at the end of each day, or at the end of our stay in each of the hotels we visit?'

His eyes narrowed. He pointed a long finger at her across the table. 'All I said was—and I mean it—that I want concentrated work with no distractions. Is that clear? I'll take a look at your reports whenever I wish—and certainly at the end of our stay at each hotel. I have no doubt whatever that you're a very conscientious secretary in the confines of an office or a hotel reception area. But to all appearances, and especially to men like Mr Collins, you're on holiday. This, coupled with your undoubted attractiveness, will lay you open to a good many temptations, and I reserve the right to remind you of your duties whenever I feel it necessary. And now shall we order our lunch?'

Lucille could have hit him! Presumably he could say whatever he liked, while she was expected to behave like the perfect secretary and just say, 'yes, sir', and 'no, sir'. She hovered between reminding him that she was a linguist, not merely a secretary, or quitting the job this very minute. But a waiter hovered near, and she had to concentrate on the menu. Then the minute they had ordered, Blair began to outline his plans for the afternoon. They were to visit the Rijksmuseum, the Historical Museum, Anne Frank's house and the Van Gogh Museum.

Her interest was captured in spite of her annoyance with him, but she determined not to let it show too much.

'It all sounds fascinating,' she observed coolly, 'but what have these visits to do with your hotel business?'

'*Our* hotel business,' he corrected. 'It will all be useful for your report, never fear, and will be needed for advertising purposes. Amsterdam is one of the most interesting cities in the world, and I intend to make our advertisements as attractive as possible. You'll be of help in writing the script for holiday brochures.'

'Are you going in for the tourist trade only? Just holiday and tourist hotels?'

'Not necessarily, but some will be, of course. It depends on the location.'

'Why not—"A hotel in every city in the world"?' Lucille suggested with sarcasm.

But her sarcasm was lost on the business mind of Blair Saunders. 'That's a *very* good idea. That shall be exactly our aim, and I'll pass it on to our advertising manager,' he said.

Lucille gave up. It was an impossible idea, anyway, but she had no doubt that her boss would have a good try.

As soon as they had eaten they went out, and a most interesting and enjoyable afternoon it turned out to be. Lucille determined that she would visit Amsterdam again at the first opportunity, also to learn the language. She knew a smattering, but that was all. She had found that so many Dutch businessmen whom she encountered in the London hotel could speak good English that after

French and German, she had gone on to Italian and Spanish. She was currently learning Japanese. Chinese had been her next target, then possibly Russian.

Being a lover of art, and particularly of Rembrandt, she found the Rijksmuseum fascinating. So, too, the Stadelijk Museum which housed important collections of Van Gogh's work. Blair surprised her by showing himself to be very knowledgeable about art. Lucille knew only when she found a painting pleasing, but Blair pointed out the painstaking workmanship, the fine brush strokes and the colour mixes which gave the various results.

'Do you paint yourself?' she asked curiously.

'When I can spare the time,' he answered rather distantly.

'Sometimes you have to make time for an activity which appears to be—non-productive,' she ventured.

He made no reply, and after a minute or two she glanced at his face, and again was surprised at the expression written there: the same tension as before, but this time coupled with a hint of pain in his dark eyes. What drove him to this everlasting pursuit of business? she wondered. What was the use of making more and more money?

From the Stadelijk Museum they made their way to the house of Anne Frank, the young Jewish girl who had written a diary while hiding from the Nazis during the German occupation and persecution of the Jews.

'I believe,' Blair remarked as they climbed the stairs, 'that there were somewhere in the region of eight thousand Jews in Amsterdam at that time—1940—and almost seventy thousand died in concentration camps. About twelve thousand went into hiding, and out of those about seven thousand survived. Anne Frank was one of those who didn't.'

It sounded grim. Lucille knew something of the history of the Second World War, of course, but not those kind of details.

'1940 sounds so long ago, although I don't suppose it seems so to those older people who can remember it. But do you really think people visiting Amsterdam on holiday will want to know about such awful times, or be reminded of them? Isn't the war best forgotten?'

'There are some who hold to that point of view,' Blair answered, 'but I'm not at all sure myself. It should be forgotten in that people of different nationalities shouldn't bear grudges because of the past. But the human race should certainly not forget what wars can do to people. In all disasters—earthquakes, volcanic eruptions, floods, as well as war, while a good many people display great bravery, there are others who will take advantage to loot, plunder, or demand large sums of money from those they assist. Wartime Amsterdam had its heroes, but it also had its cowards and its greedy and indifferent people.'

'Yes, but——'

'And to answer your question,' he interrupted, 'as to whether visitors to Amsterdam will want to see places like the Anne Frank house, and be reminded of those times, I think the answer is yes. If it's not on the itinerary they'll want to know why.'

Lucille was surprised at the understanding he showed of human nature, of his assessment of human behaviour, and his sympathy for those persecuted and in distress.

Upstairs was a bust of the young girl, the room and the tiny space in which she had remained cooped up, kept bare in her memory. Blair was right, Lucille thought. It was well to know and to remember what people had had to suffer, and the endurance and courage of which mankind could be capable.

Somehow this conversation with Blair gave her a fresh insight into his character. Perhaps he was not as mercenary as he seemed. He was certainly taking pains to investigate the hotels he was interested in buying—at least, so far. Perhaps she had misjudged him. Perhaps he was as much interested in giving a service as in making money.

'You're very quiet,' he observed later, when they were having afternoon tea on the hotel terrace. 'Is anything wrong?'

As he had been the object of her thoughts, Lucille found her cheeks grew warm.

'No, no,' she answered swiftly, 'nothing's wrong.'

'Good,' he said briskly. 'Perhaps when we've had tea, you wouldn't mind completing your report and letting me have it this evening. And you'll need some time for your packing. I want to make an early start in the morning. So we'll have dinner, then go on this so-called romantic candlelight cruise.'

Lucille detected a certain cynicism in his voice, and she heartily disliked cynics. They always saw the worst in things and people. Her new opinion of him received a slight setback.

'Why do you say "so-called"?' she challenged. 'Is there no room in your life for romance?'

His eyes narrowed, and she knew she had taken a great liberty in speaking so to him.

'What is romance?' he countered. 'Tell me that—if you're such an expert.'

'I—I don't know that I *am* an expert,' she answered defensively. 'And it's rather difficult to define. But I imagine there *is* something about soft lights and sweet music which relaxes people, and if they're in the company of someone they love—young people or married couples—well then, their thoughts and feelings for each other are—intensified.'

'Mm,' he almost grunted in a sceptical tone, 'you *are* a romantic, aren't you? And do these "feelings" you speak of evaporate when the said couples step off the launch or begin the real business of everyday life?'

'Not necessarily.'

'But nine times out of ten.'

Lucille gave an exasperated sigh and put down her half-finished tea. 'You really are impossible!' she said recklessly, and rose to her feet. 'I think if you don't mind, I'll go and finish my report now, and maybe sort out my belongings ready to pack later on.'

Blair's shoulders lifted. 'Do whatever you like,' he said with such marked indifference she could have hit him.

Fuming, she climbed the stairs instead of taking the lift. The man is impossible! she said to herself, flinging her handbag on the bed. What his idea was of dragging her out on the candlelight cruise this evening if he was so cynical, she really didn't know. Then she pulled herself up. Surely she hadn't expected—and wanted—him to feel romantic? They were going simply to see whether or not the cruise was good value for money. At least, she supposed that was the idea.

Her report did not take long to complete. If necessary, she could add a word or two about the cruise later. She had a bath, and feeling suddenly sleepy, lay on the bed and closed her eyes. Inevitably her thoughts strayed to her boss. What a contradictory man he was! She really didn't know whether she liked him or not. At times she admired him, such as this afternoon, but more often than not he infuriated her. She thought of the candlelight cruise, and unconsciously tried to imagine what it would be like to have romantic feelings about him. All around, she supposed, there would be couples holding hands, looking into each other's eyes, exchanging loving glances, even kissing. Would Blair ever——

CHAPTER FOUR

A SUDDEN KNOCKING brought her out of her thoughts. She glanced at her watch and realised that she had slept for some hours. She slipped on her dressing-gown to see a waitress standing there who reminded her that Mr Saunders was awaiting her at the dinner table. Lucille thanked her and dressed swiftly, putting on only the lightest of make-up.

Blair rose as she arrived at table, and it was difficult to know from his inscrutable expression whether he was annoyed or not at being kept waiting.

'I do apologise,' she said swiftly. 'I fell asleep. Have you been waiting long?'

'Not so very long,' he answered. 'All the same, I think we should go straight on to the main course, otherwise we shall have to gulp everything down in order not to be late.'

Feeling suitably rebuked, Lucille nodded. 'I—finished my report on the hotel, the shopping facilities and our afternoon visits,' she told him. 'If you wish, I can add a few words about tonight's excursion later.'

'Very well, but I would like to see it tonight. That will give me time to read it and add my own comments before we move on to the next place.'

'Yes, of course. May I ask where we're going next?'

'To Paris—and it's a good day's drive. I want to arrive in time for an evening meal, so please don't be late down to breakfast.'

Lucille felt as though she'd received a slap in the face. And this time she did not feel angry, only hurt.

'Was that really necessary?' she asked him quietly after a moment or two.

'Was what necessary? Of course——'

'I don't make a habit of being unpunctual,' she reminded him. 'Just say what time you want to depart and what time you would like me to be down for breakfast, and I'll be here all right.'

His eyes flickered. 'You'll not oversleep?'

'No, I'll set my alarm.'

'Good.'

No apology for being rude and unreasonable, of course. That would be too much to expect, her thoughts went while she tackled the steak he had ordered.

They ate in silence for a while until Lucille could stand it no longer. Blair did not seem to be in a very good mood this evening, still less a romantic one. Perhaps he was beginning to regret his decision to go on the candle-light cruise. But then if that was the case he would simply cancel it.

'How many hotels—and what grade—are we staying in, in Paris?' she ventured.

'Two,' he informed her, after a pause. 'One on the Left Bank, the other in the city centre. One night, I think, will be sufficient in the one on the Left Bank. We'll stay two nights in the other.'

'Do you expect to buy them both?' she asked incredulously.

He shrugged. 'They're an offer. Whether I buy them or not depends upon your report—at least largely. In any case, your expectations, should I say your standards, might differ from mine.'

This needled her somewhat. 'And what exactly do you mean by that?' she demanded.

Blair met her angry look with complete indifference. 'I simply meant that your requirements might be more—modest than mine, and, of course, I want to cater for all tastes. Not everyone, for example, could afford to stay at our hotel in London. Nor, I imagine, the second one we shall be staying in, in Paris.'

But his explanation did not mollify her, although she realised what he meant.

'And so you think I don't appreciate first-class food, first-class service and elegant surroundings?'

'I didn't say that,' he answered smoothly. 'Please don't put interpretations on what I say that I don't intend.'

'It's difficult to know sometimes what you *do* intend,' she told him.

'That you must sort out for yourself,' he answered as a waiter hovered near.

His arrogance, Lucille thought to herself, was sometimes beyond belief, and this was one of the times. However, as the dessert trolley appeared, there was nothing further she could say for a few minutes, and by the time they had been served she decided to say nothing.

As she had anticipated, most of the other passengers on the candlelight cruise were young couples, some looking distinctly dewy-eyed and romantic, others giving a giggle or two, and some older people appearing a little embarrassed and in most cases covering up their embarrassment by talking over-loudly or pretending to be romantic and failing dismally. Blair and Lucille sat at a table for two, lit of course by candles, and as the launch began to move some music permeated everywhere, and waiters moved from table to table serving wine and cheeses.

It really could be romantic, Lucille acknowledged with a certain wistfulness. As they glided smoothly along the lights of the city were reflected in the water, and the whole atmosphere was most relaxing. The young couples began to hold hands, the older ones stopped their loud talking and spoke in softer tones and were obviously enjoying the trip. Lucille stole a glance at Blair, but his attention was fixed upon the passing scenery. Lucille sipped the wine and nibbled her cheese, both of which were extremely pleasant, and blended perfectly together.

Then she found Blair looking at her, a soft half-smile on his usually tight lips.

'Feeling romantic yet?' he asked, keeping his voice low.

'It's—difficult not to when everyone else around is so obviously feeling sentimental,' she answered.

'Oh, well, in that case——'

He reached across the table and took her hand and, ridiculously, her heart missed a beat. His touch was firm and cool and she liked the feel of it. She would have liked to stay that way, but she could not pretend a romantic feeling which was not there. After a minute or two she made an effort to free her hand, and he let it go.

'Wrong person?' he quizzed sarcastically.

'I—can't pretend something I don't feel,' she answered.

'I didn't want you to,' he came back swiftly. 'Only to go through the motions.'

'Well, I can't do that either.'

'Very well. Perhaps you'd prefer to hold hands with a waiter. There's a very good-looking one over there,' said Blair with undoubted sarcasm, looking in the direction of a young, fair-haired waiter.

Lucille compressed her lips. Because he was her employer, he obviously thought he could say anything he liked to her. Was the money she was going to earn on this assignment going to be worth the continual blunt edge of his tongue, his insults and his sarcasm? She looked at the young waiter. For a moment he was gazing out of the window at the brilliance of the passing lights and their jewelled reflection in the dark waters of the canal.

'Yes, he is quite good-looking,' she conceded.

'If you like the type,' answered Blair.

'How does one know what "type" a person is until one gets to know them?'

'You don't, of course.'

'Exactly,' she retorted. 'And I don't hold hands with anyone I don't—don't know well enough,' she finished. She had almost said 'don't like', but that would have been too honest.

There was a long silence. Lucille looked determinedly out of the large windows. She was almost certain that he had guessed what she had been going to say. Well, it served him right, she thought unrepentantly. In any case, she had no doubt that the feeling was mutual. It had been a ridiculous idea to come on this cruise. She tried not to feel envious of the loving couples all around them, but was glad when at last it was over and they were walking back to the hotel.

'Well, and what did you think of it?' asked Blair as they neared the hotel. 'Romantic enough with the right person?'

'Oh yes, very,' she answered briefly, then added, 'Shouldn't be missed.'

He gave a noncommittal grunt, and when they had collected their keys from Reception they said goodnight.

Feeling somewhat ragged, Lucille packed all but her night things and the suit she intended wearing on tomorrow's journey. This done, she finished her report and read for a while. She tried not to look at the communicating door which separated her from Blair, but when she put out her own light at close on midnight, she could not help noticing that his was still on. It was only then that she remembered he had wanted her report tonight. With a startled exclamation she put on her light again and reached for her dressing-gown. He was probably waiting for it. What was the matter with her these days? Why did she keep having to apologise to him?

Nothing would have induced her to knock on the communicating door. In any case, he had said he had left the key at Reception. So there was nothing for it but to go and knock on his door next to hers in the corridor. She only hoped that no one would see her knocking at this hour.

She knocked and waited, then had to knock again, hoping he hadn't gone to sleep, after all, and left his light on. After a few moments, however, it opened and he stood there in a dark green silk dressing gown.

'Well—hello,' he said in a faintly surprised tone.

Lucille handed him her folder containing her report. 'I'm—most terribly sorry, I—I forgot to bring it sooner.' Somehow the sight of him standing there looking so male and at the same time elegant unnerved her.

'What is it?' he asked.

Aggravating man! Surely he knew? Her cheeks felt warm as he looked her up and down. She had put on her dressing-gown hurriedly in her agitation and could feel it slipping open. It was only flimsy at best.

'It's my report on the hotel you said you wanted.'

He glanced pointedly at his watch. 'It's taken you a long time to bring it. How did you know I wasn't in bed and asleep?'

Lucille thrust the report in his hands and let it go. 'I could see your light on under the other door,' she told him. 'And I've already said I'm sorry.'

'Well, you shouldn't have to keep apologising, should you?'

'I'm aware of that!' she flashed back, and not wishing to dally any longer, she muttered goodnight through her teeth and went back to her room. What an impossible man he was turning out to be, she thought angrily, as she slipped back into bed again. Why couldn't he just have accepted the report and her apology with a simple word of thanks? If she had known there was going to be this continual conflict she would never have taken on this job. What did he want with all these hotels anyway, and why ask her to accompany him? Why ask anyone? He could quite easily have visited them himself or even have sent an agent or someone. Drat the man!

She was so disturbed and annoyed she found great difficulty getting to sleep, and twice checked that she had set her travel alarm clock for morning. At this rate it would be morning before she got to sleep. She was still tossing when Blair's light went out, and though she did not realise it at the time all she could see in her mind's eye was the way he had looked in his dressing gown. Every inch a man, and an exciting one at that. She scarcely knew whether she was angry with herself or whether it was directed against him.

It seemed she had only just closed her eyes when she was awakened by her alarm. She longed to be able to turn over and let sleep overtake her once more, but she dared not. She dragged herself out of bed long before her morning tea arrived, and was down to breakfast, her luggage all ready, almost five minutes before Blair joined her.

At the sight of her waiting for him his eyebrows raised a fraction.

'Good morning,' he said. 'I trust you slept well.'

'Not very,' she answered candidly.

'Oh? Why not?'

'By the time I'd delivered the report to you, I was wide awake.'

'Pity,' was his brief comment.

He was probably thinking it had been her own fault. 'What did you think of the report?' she asked.

'Quite adequate, and very useful.'

Condemned by faint praise, thought Lucille. 'And have you decided the hotel is worth buying?'

'I haven't decided anything yet. These kind of deals are not done in a hurry. I shall wait to see what some of the others are like.'

'But supposing that while you're making up your mind, some of those you really want are snapped up by a rival hotelier?'

'Don't worry,' he said smoothly, 'I usually get what I want in the end.'

Lucille felt sure he did. 'I notice you said "usually",' she said reflectively. 'Does that mean that you don't always?'

He nodded. 'But so often I find that on the occasions that I lose, it wasn't worth the winning, anyway.'

'You're sure you don't think yourself into that view in order to boost your self-esteem?' she asked boldly.

'Quite sure. Now, if you've finished your breakfast, we'll get going, shall we?'

Feeling very much as though she had been put in her place, Lucille rose, and while Blair was settling their account, supervised the stacking of the luggage into the car.

For a long time Blair drove in silence. There was a great deal of traffic in the suburbs of Amsterdam, and Lucille did not wish to spoil his concentration by talking, so she kept silent. But when they were driving along the motorway which led directly to Paris, she did venture to engage him in conversation.

'Did you like Amsterdam? But then I expect you've been many times before.'

'I have, yes,' he answered. 'But I still like it. For many people its attraction lies in the fact that it's different from most other cities. Except Venice, of course. But we had a similar conversation on the way to Amsterdam, so if you must talk choose a more original subject, will you?'

'Perhaps it would be better if you chose one,' she answered, feeling nettled.

'I just want to concentrate on my driving,' he told her.

Lucille sighed. 'You'd rather I didn't talk at all?'

'Not necessarily.'

He really was the most aggravating man! He would drive any woman clean out of her mind in a very short space of time. That was, if he ever found a woman fool enough to marry him. Though she supposed many women might be tempted to marry him for his money.

After a long silence in which she was busy with her thoughts, he asked: 'Well, can't you find a suitable subject?'

'For what?' she asked, so startled by his question that she didn't know to what he was referring for a moment.

'For conversation, of course.'

'Oh, that. I'm afraid I was deep in thought and wasn't thinking of a subject to talk about.'

'Really? Well, why not tell me what you were thinking?'

Heavens, what a catastrophe that would be! she thought. What on earth could she say to him that would not sound highly indelicate, not to mention impertinent?

'I—wasn't thinking of anything in particular,' she hedged.

'Come now, I can't believe that. What do women think about when their minds are not specifically occupied? The men—or man—in their lives?'

He was nearer the truth than he knew. But she was not to be drawn.

'And what do men think about when they're engaged in an activity which doesn't take up all of their minds?' she came back. 'The women in their lives? Or, in your case, just business and where they can make the most money?'

The long silence told her she had probably caught him on the raw.

At last he said cynically, 'Sometimes it's more pleasant to dwell on the prospect of money-making than it is on the women in one's life. Does that satisfy you?'

'It doesn't surprise me.'

'Of course not. You've thoroughly made up your mind about me, haven't you?'

This thrust brought the colour to her cheeks. She had a sneaking feeling that she was judging him too harshly.

He continued, before she could reply, 'Not that it worries me what you think, but in our line of business it's not a good idea to make hasty judgements of people. It may land you in difficulties. Besides which, it's bad for business.'

Bad for business. Lucille clung on to the phrase which served to stave off his accusation that she was guilty of making hasty judgements of people, and of himself in particular. He was right, of course. Most people made misjudgements at some time in their lives, and she counted herself no exception, although she had always secretly felt herself to be a reasonably good judge of character, making certain allowances for human frailty. All the same, Blair's opinion irked her and she tried to thrust it away from her in criticism of him, and deep down she was hurt by his remark, *'Not that it worries me what you think'*. They were destined, it seemed, to be antagonists.

There was a long silence, broken only by a halt for a coffee at a service station on the motorway followed by another silent drive until they made a stop for lunch. It was Blair who broke the silence.

'I presume you've already been to Paris?' he asked.

'When I was learning the language—yes. I had two months.'

'And where did you stay?'

'At one of the student hostels in the Boulevard St-Michel. It was summer and the students were on holiday.'

'And what was the accommodation like there?'

'Clean, but otherwise basic. Just a bed, a table and a chair. No restaurant, of course.'

She was aware how stiff and unfriendly her voice must sound, and wondered fleetingly whether her boss would notice.

'Yes, I know the type. Well, the place we're going to will be almost as basic, and as you may know, a good many of the hotels over here have no restaurant. But there are usually one or two quite near.'

His voice sounded stilted too, and Lucille was finding it most unpleasant.

'I thought you were only going for first-class hotels,' she remarked.

'In the main I am, but one must also cater for the young who want to travel but whose income is limited. It's better by far to provide them with good clean accommodation and let them search around for food in the different cafés, rather than supply a multi-storey monstrosity with cheap food badly cooked and with discos and such like thrown in.'

Lucille couldn't agree with him more, for many reasons, not least in that young people were trying to learn the language, but she felt she had to make a better contribution to their conversation than simply agreeing.

'But some young people might like that kind of hotel— if all they need is a fun holiday.'

'Then someone else can provide it, but not the Blair Saunders enterprises,' was his answer. 'I want to buy good four- or five-star hotels or quiet, inexpensive ones which just give good basic accommodation.'

'And will you change the names of the ones you buy?'

'I hadn't thought about it. What do you think?'

Lucille was quite taken aback for a moment. 'I'm not sure. I suppose if it's a really good hotel, and you're satisfied with the service, etc., then regular clients will have become accustomed to the old name. If not, but you still would like to buy for any reason and improve the facilities, then it might be a good idea to change the name. Or better still, if you want a name to become symbolic of good service, you could first establish a name, then change the others gradually.'

'And what name would you suggest?'

'Why not—the Blair Saunders?'

He eyed her suspiciously. 'Are you serious?'

'Why not? Your name would then become known throughout the world.'

'Perhaps I don't want my name to become known all over the world. It can cause problems.'

'Is that why you registered at the Hotel International under the name of Gregory?' she asked, suddenly remembering.

'That's right.'

'Why Gregory? That doesn't sound right for you, somehow.'

'For hotel names, you mean, perhaps. It's my mother's maiden name. I often use it.'

'I see. But I still think it would be a good idea to have all the hotels under the same name. That way, you'd build up a reputation.' Lucille gave a little mischievous smile. 'You could still use your mother's name or any other if you wanted to visit any of the hotels incognito.'

He gave her an odd look. 'I think I shall have to put you on the board of directors! You'd do very well.'

She was so unused to serious compliments from him, and the suggestion was so improbable she was sure he was indulging in sarcasm again at her expense.

'No, thank you,' she told him decisively, adding, 'I think by the time this trip is over, I shall have had my fill of hotels. Maybe I shall look around for a job as interpreter—which was my intention in the first place.'

She saw his expression harden, and knew she had said the wrong thing. For the rest of the journey he scarcely spoke, and she was glad when at last they arrived at the hotel on the Left Bank of the Seine. They settled in and found a nearby restaurant for their evening meal, and the only consolation Lucille had was that her French was indisputably better than Blair's. After they had eaten, he saw her back to the hotel and left her, saying he was going to take a walk. It was ten-thirty, anyway, and so Lucille decided to go to bed. But she felt an extraordinary flatness. She had to admit that she would have liked to stroll around the streets of Paris with him. Why did she have to give him the impression that she was already fed up with the hotel business? She wasn't, really. She had chosen hotel work because she liked meeting people. So why had she said it? A reaction against Blair? That they were not getting along very well together?

Whichever way it was, she felt restless and out of sorts. She changed her mind about going straight to bed. She doubted whether she would be able to sleep and she had nothing suitable to read at the moment. So she changed into a pair of jeans and a sloppy sweater and set off for a café she knew—or used to know—quite near. She might even come across some of the young French people she had made friends with when she was here as a language student.

She reached the café, where she ordered a coffee and glanced all around for a familiar face or two, but saw none. There were the usual street vendors trying to sell dirty postcards, 'gold' watches, bracelets and the like, but nowhere did she see anyone she knew. Three youths came and sat at the table she occupied, and after a while one of them began to talk to her. At first she answered them politely, but then they began to make the kind of suggestions she did not care for. She rose and decided she had better get back to the hotel.

She had not gone far, however, when she was suddenly attacked from behind. An arm came around her throat, then she felt both legs being lifted from the ground.

'Let me go!' she shouted in French. 'Let me go!'

But raucous laughter was the only answer. The arm around her throat slid under her arms and she was lifted bodily and rushed into a nearby alley. She struggled and shouted with all the force she could muster. Then a hand closed over her mouth and she found herself being forced on to the ground. Their intention was all too clear. One of them clawed at the zip of her jeans. She struggled violently and managed to jab her elbow hard into the stomach of the one whose hand was over her mouth.

'Blair—Blair, come quick!' she yelled at the top of her voice. He might be miles away, but she had to shout something.

'Keep quiet or I'll knock you senseless,' one of them said, but it was with great satisfaction that she heard a moan of pain from the one she had jabbed.

She kicked out and moved her head from side to side to prevent another hand from silencing her while she continued to shout Blair's name.

The next moment she was given a vicious punch. She screamed as her head hit the ground, and then darkness closed over her.

When she recovered consciousness she was in bed, and Blair was leaning over her anxiously.

'Blair——' Without realising what she was doing she put up her hand and touched his face.

His hand closed over hers before gently removing it and laying it on the counterpane.

'Thank goodness you've come round at last!' he said in a relieved tone. 'How do you feel?'

Lucille winced. 'Except for where my head banged the ground—all right, I think.'

He straightened. 'Thank goodness for that! The doctor should be here any minute. But what on earth possessed you to go out on your own? Surely you know that the streets of Paris are not safe for a woman on her own?'

'But when I was here before——'

'That was years ago. It's not safe even in our country, more's the pity. When I think of what might have happened to you if I hadn't happened to come along——'

'Did—did you hear me calling?' she asked him.

'I heard a scream. I had no idea it was you until——'

The door opened and the hotel manageress came in, followed by a man whom Madame introduced as the doctor. After a few words of explanation about what had happened, he examined the swelling on the back of Lucille's head, tested her eyes and their reaction to light and felt her throat.

'Well,' he said, 'I don't think much damage has been done. I take it that you, *monsieur*,' he looked at Blair, 'arrived on the scene soon enough to prevent the young lady from being—how you say—assaulted?'

'Just about,' Blair answered grimly. 'Fortunately, she has a good pair of lungs.'

'I kick pretty hard too,' Lucille put in.

Blair's eyes blazed as he swung round and pointed a finger at her. 'This is no joke—and it must never happen again. You hear?'

Surprised at his anger, she nevertheless faced him squarely. 'Short of never walking the streets of Paris, or any other city, at night, I don't see that it can be prevented from happening again. I simply refuse to be kept a prisoner!'

He gave an exasperated sigh. 'You know perfectly well what I mean. From now on, you don't go out alone after dark. Is that clearly understood?'

'Oh yes, it's clear enough,' she answered. 'But I'd like to make one or two things clear too. I refuse to have my freedom curtailed. Obviously, if I'm left alone and I want to go out, I have no option but to go by myself. I can well understand that having been in my company all day, you will—or may—not want it also in the evening. And *vice versa*, of course.'

Blair gave her a hard look. 'I repeat—and this is irrespective of what I do want or don't want—you are not to go out alone at night ever again while we're on this trip. And that is final.'

'And if I don't?'

'You go on the very next plane to London.'

Lucille knew a swift anger. 'As a matter of fact, that will——' *suit me just fine,* she had been going to say, but a sudden pain shot through the wound in her head, and she winced.

'I think you'd better rest,' Blair said at once. 'If you're sure she's in no danger, doctor——' The doctor shook his head and muttered a couple of negatives. 'In that case,' Blair went on, 'I think we'd all better leave her.' He ushered them out, but at the door he turned. 'You should sleep the night through but if you have any nightmares, or you need anything, my room is just a little way along the corridor—number nine. Don't forget, now.'

Her anger died. He was trying to be kind. She shook her head, half in despair of ever understanding him. 'I won't,' she promised.

She turned on her side and put out the light. He was quite right, really; she shouldn't have gone out alone. This was a restless age, a violent age, and young men in groups or gangs were often tempted to make various kinds of attacks on females on their own. If only Blair wouldn't be so high-handed about everything!

She was just beginning to awaken the next morning when a knock came on her door. Still half asleep, she called out 'come in', and half expected to see the manageress with a cup of tea, but when the door opened Blair stood there.

'How did you sleep?' he asked.

'Oh, I——' she struggled to sit up, 'er—very well, actually.'

'Do you feel fit to come out for some breakfast?'

Suddenly she felt shy of him and pulled up the bed-clothes to her chin. 'Yes, of course.'

'Good. I'll wait for you downstairs,' he said briskly, and went out again, having scarcely looked at her.

Lucille sighed and got out of bed. She would have loved a long soak in the bath, but a quick shower would have to do. She couldn't in all conscience keep him waiting any longer than necessary.

He was waiting for her in the small foyer. 'You feeling all right now?' he asked immediately.

She nodded. 'I was lucky that you came along when you did,' she said. 'I realise now that I couldn't have fought the three of them for much longer. I'm—sorry. You were quite right about my not going out alone at night.'

He acknowledged her apology with a slight smile. Lucille interpreted it as one of triumph, and almost wished she had not bothered.

They had coffee and croissants at a small café at the top of the street, and after a while Blair asked:

'What do you think of the hotel?'

She shrugged her shoulders. 'It's adequate. The beds are clean and comfortable—at least, mine was,' she amended, 'so I'm presuming that was the general standard. There was also plenty of hot water. I'll write up my report after breakfast.'

He thought for a moment, then surprised her by asking, 'Do you think we should buy it?'

It always surprised her when he used the word 'we' instead of 'I'—as though she was an old-established, senior member of the firm. It surprised her, too, to be asked her opinion.

'Since you ask me, no, I don't think you—er—we should buy it,' she answered.

'Why not?'

'Well, I think you——' Lucille simply could not get used to saying 'we'—'should buy only first-class hotels—

four- or five-star. That is, if you want to build up a good reputation. The "A hotel in every city in the world" idea. Of course, it will be generally assumed that you mean every *major* city. Clean, comfortable and plenty of hot water is only basic.'

'And you think we should aim at a little more than basics.'

She nodded. 'A lot more.'

'Mm—very interesting. Perhaps when you write your reports it would be a good idea for you to add your recommendations. For example: buy. Or: don't buy. Or even any alterations you would recommend.'

She eyed him suspiciously. Was he being sarcastic? If he was, she decided to take him at his word.

'Very well, I'll do that,' she agreed.

Blair decided they should book into the next hotel in time to have lunch there, so after a short walk along the fascinating Boulevard St-Germain where artists sold their pictures and visitors of all nationalities gathered, they went back to the hotel and packed their overnight bags. Blair drove to the other side of the river to the Right Bank, which was supposed to epitomise wealth and good taste, couture clothes, credit cards and traffic jams, secretaries and long-distance phone calls.

'There's so much to see in Paris,' said Blair as they crossed the Place de la Concorde. 'But I expect you've seen most of what there is, haven't you?'

'Pretty nearly, but there are some places one never tires of visiting.'

'Such as?'

'The Montmartre area.'

'Of course.'

Their hotel was just off the Champs-Elysées. Parking was no problem. No sooner had Blair drawn up outside the quite splendid-looking place than a porter appeared to take their luggage. It was when they were greeted by the receptionist that Lucille received the shock.

'*Ah, oui*—Monsieur et Madame Saunders. Your suite—it is all ready for you.'

CHAPTER FIVE

'OUR SUITE!' gasped Lucille, turning furious eyes on Blair. 'I told you——'

He gave her a warning look. 'Come and see, and argue afterwards,' he told her in a quiet voice. 'But please don't make a scene in public.'

Keys were being handed to the porter who was loading their luggage on to a trolley. Blair put his hand under her elbow and led her to the lift. Lucille burned with anger, but held her tongue for the moment. He was not going to get away with this! In no way was she going to share rooms with him. It might be done in his circle, but not in hers. He had no right to do this, especially without telling her.

The suite of rooms was the last word in luxury and elegance. It almost took Lucille's breath away, as the porter showed them the beautifully styled bedroom and bathroom, the small dressing-room and the sitting-room with a balcony which overlooked a green park.

'I will send up a chambermaid to help Madame with her unpacking,' said the bowing porter as Blair pressed a generous tip into his palm.

'That's quite all right,' Lucille interposed swiftly. 'I do *not* need any help, thank you.'

She had every intention of demanding a separate room just as soon as the porter had gone. If Blair would not agree, she would either see the management herself or catch the next plane to London.

As soon as the door closed behind the porter she turned furious eyes on Blair.

'I will not share this suite with you! There is absolutely no need——'

His eyes were wide with anger, too. 'For goodness' sake, you ridiculous woman, what does it matter? Why must you be such a prude?'

'I'm *not* a prude!' she stormed. 'It might not matter to you, but it matters a great deal to me with whom I share a—a room.'

'With whom you share a bed, you mean, don't you?' he came back with icy scorn.

'All right, then, yes. With whom I share a bed,' she answered.

'I am not asking you to share a bed with me,' he said slowly and with insulting emphasis.

'It's—the same thing,' she answered lamely.

'It's not the same thing at all,' he assured her smoothly. 'To begin with, there are twin beds. I wouldn't like to have to share a single bed with anyone—most uncomfortable, not enough room to turn over. Pyjamas or nightdresses, or whatever it is you wear, are respectable enough. You'd be as safe at a distance of a few feet as you would be a few miles. And if you're all that worried I can take a mattress and bedding into the dressing-room and sleep there. Satisfied?'

There was something stirring within her that she could not quite analyse, did not want to analyse. She was afraid to.

'But—but I don't do this kind of thing,' she protested.

'I'm glad to hear it.'

'Then why do you expect me to do it with you?'

'It's a matter of business, that's all.'

'But I don't see—— And there's the staff. What are they going to think?'

Blair's lips twitched slightly. 'They think we're married,' he said casually. 'You wouldn't have them think otherwise, would you?'

He appeared to have her cornered. She began to feel she was making a fuss about nothing. What was she afraid of? He was not the kind of man to rape a woman, she was sure of that. Perhaps she was afraid of herself. And it was not very flattering the way he kept intimating that he did not—and would not—find her the least bit tempting.

'I—could ring down to the manager and ask to be given a single room,' she told him with a feeling that she was making a last desperate stand in the sure knowledge that she would not win.

Blair shook his head at her. 'Now what good do you think that will do? It will merely focus attention on both of us, you in particular, and will make them think there's something wrong. Far better leave things as they are. I want you to have the experience of a suite like this, to report on it, to demand service—anything you want— and test the response you receive. I'm in the hotel business, and I want a woman's reaction. Just behave as though I'm not here. All right?'

Lucille gave in. There was still something not quite right about it, but she felt she could argue against his logic no more. She took another look around the room. She could never in a million years afford to pay what this suite must be costing.

Blair watched her. 'You must admit it's a cut above the place where we stayed last night.'

She laughed shortly. 'There's no denying that.'

He took a step nearer to her, and her instinctive re- action was to step backwards. Why, she didn't know, but she stopped herself just in time.

'Why don't you just relax,' he told her. 'Pretend you've won a prize in some competition which entitles you to a couple of days' holiday at "a luxury hotel". Or pretend you're a woman of means. Who knows, you might be one day.'

'That's hardly likely,' she answered stiffly.

Feeling unaccountably stifled in his presence, she wandered back into the bedroom. A deep-pile carpet covered the floor from wall to wall. Across the whole of one wall was a double wardrobe and dressing-table; the lamps on each bedside table were of lead crystal in a warm wine colour with deeply faceted cuts and cross-cuts. The plinths and carriages were of rich golden burnished brass intricately patterned. Lucille could imagine the brilliance when they were switched on. The bedcovers were of richly embroidered tapestry, and she guessed that the sheets would be equally luxurious. The two armchairs looked like antiques, as did the various ornaments. The bathroom was spacious, with separate shower, beautiful fittings and large, soft towels. Was this really how the other half lived? What was Blair's home like, if he took this kind of opulence for granted?

She wandered back into the sitting-room with its fine furniture, thick carpet, the Dresden china figures on the Adam—or Adam-style—fireplace. It was very, very pleasant and charming indeed. Blair was standing on the balcony looking out across the park, and turned as she entered the room.

'Well? Do you like it?' he asked.

'Of course. Who wouldn't?'

'Precisely, so I suggest you make the most of it. Now, let's go down and sample their food and see if we can pick holes in the service, shall we? Then you can tell me what you'd like to do for the rest of the day.'

'Why ask me?' Lucille couldn't resist rejoining. 'You never have before.'

'Well, I am now,' he came back bluntly. 'So stop being so damned difficult!'

It was the nearest thing to reminding her that he was her employer, and she felt guilty.

'Just give me a moment to tidy up, will you?' she asked.

'Naturally.'

She washed her hands and renewed her make-up, the feeling growing on her that her behaviour and attitude towards Blair was wrong somehow. She had never felt so unsettled, so easily put out, so argumentative. She really must remember that she was here to do a job of work, that Blair was paying her very good money to do as he asked. He was even, she supposed, entitled to be difficult, whereas she wasn't.

The restaurant could only be described as sumptuous. Lucille had never seen anything like it. As they were ushered to their table with great ceremony, she did her best to appear as though such a place was commonplace to her. The lighting was superb, banks of flowers were everywhere and the tables gleamed with spotless table-cloths, cut glass wine glasses and silver cutlery. Immediately after they were seated, huge menus were put into their hands.

'Impressed?' asked Blair, his eyes flicking around the place.

'Oh yes, certainly.'

'Not overwhelmed?'

'Should I be?' she countered.

He gave her a thoughtful look. 'No, not necessarily. And you don't look it. Congratulations. You're beginning to get accustomed to such surroundings already. That's good.'

'Is it?'

'Certainly. Now, what would you like to eat?'

The menu was daunting. Lucille felt a sudden desire to giggle as she wondered what Blair's reaction—not to mention that of the waiter—would be if she asked for fish and chips.

'I think, on the whole, I'll leave it to you,' she told him.

'You know, of course, that the French are absolute fanatics about their food.'

'Yes, I know. They'll take a whole evening over it.'

'And half the evening deciding what to have and discussing it with the waiter. I shall probably need your help with my French.'

The waiter duly came, and there followed a discussion to the point of a conversation on each item on the menu, with absurd gesticulations from the waiter on the gastronomic delights of each item. At last they had decided on the first three courses, and close on the waiter's heels came the wine waiter, with another long discussion on wines.

'If this is the standard for lunch, I wonder what dinner will be like,' remarked Lucille. 'I should think it will be hard to fault the food in a place like this in France. Some of the top chefs, I understand, acquire a sort of "star" status. There's a story about one chef—now famous— who shocked his customers by actually cooking his fish in red wine, then serving it with a red wine sauce. It simply wasn't done to serve fish with red wine. But it was so perfect, the sauce so delicious, it became one of the most imitated dishes in Paris. He also poached the common turnip in Normandy cider and stuffed it with aromatic herbs and meats so that people's taste buds tingled and their heads reeled with joy. I—don't know whether so much preoccupation with food is a good thing or a bad one,' she finished, suddenly aware that Blair was eyeing her very oddly. 'I'm—sorry, I'm afraid I've been talking too much.'

He laughed, the first time she had heard him laugh since she had known him. 'On the contrary, what you've been saying is most entertaining. Are you a good cook yourself?'

She shrugged. 'That's not really for me to say, is it? I'm not over-fond of cooking, I'm afraid I regard it as something that has to be done if one wants to eat, but I tend to stick to simple dishes, and get it over as quickly as possible so that I can retire to the sitting-room, or whatever, and talk, or listen to others talk; or listen to music, or learn a language. Does that shock you?'

He shook his head. 'It doesn't surprise me. And suppose one day you get married—which I'm sure you will,' he added hastily, 'how will your husband fare?'

'Oh, well enough, I should think.' She grinned. 'If he's a fanatic about food, he can cook it himself if mine doesn't suit him!'

This caused him to raise his eyebrows a little. 'That sounds a very "couldn't care less" attitude for a wife to take.'

'We're talking about fanatics,' she reminded him. 'If a husband—or wife, or anyone for that matter—is such a fanatic about anything, why should they impose it on other people? Let them get on with it.'

Another raise of his brows. Lucille couldn't help feeling that she shouldn't be talking to him like this. It was not how a secretary should talk to her employer. But she was finding it increasingly difficult to draw a distinction between treating him as an ordinary man and someone who was paying her even for doing what she was at this moment—being served with lunch.

'It depends, really, how you define a fanatic,' Blair was saying. 'What's your definition?'

'We-ll, I suppose it's someone who goes to extremes, usually about something that isn't worthwhile—such as a food fad, or to do with their health—or at any rate one subject to the exclusion of all else, and no matter how it might be affecting those with whom they live.'

'But sometimes the only way to draw attention to some injustice or other good cause is to be—or appear to be—a fanatic. The suffragettes, for instance.'

'I did say something that wasn't worthwhile,' Lucille reminded him.

'So you did,' he conceded. 'But then again, what seems worthwhile to some might not to others.'

'You are splitting hairs,' she told him recklessly.

'Am I? Well, let me split them a little more. My interest lies in the hotel business, and my business is hotels. Would you call me a fanatic?'

Lucille almost choked over her smoked salmon. 'How on earth am I supposed to answer that?'

'Just be honest,' he told her. 'You're not doing badly so far.'

But Lucille scarcely knew how to begin. 'It really isn't quite the same thing,' she told him. 'It depends on your motives, for one thing. For another, it depends on what other interests you have. I don't really know you, do I?'

He grunted. 'You're becoming diplomatic all at once! I thought you'd thoroughly made up your mind about me and my motives.'

Lucille wished he'd change the subject. It had become much too personal, and she was at a loss as to why he had directed it that way. He was the most difficult and unpredictable man she had ever known.

The meal, needless to say, was one of the most perfect Lucille had ever tasted.

'You really think you'd buy a hotel like this?' she asked Blair as they went up to their suite in the lift.

'Why not?'

But she couldn't really think of a practical reason. After all, his London hotel was five-star-plus, if there was such a rating. It just wasn't quite as opulent.

'Won't it be extremely costly?'

'Yes. But think of the returns.'

'And it's on the market?'

'Not quite the open market, but I happen to know that the company who owns it is in need of finance and wants to sell off some of its hotels—whereas I want to expand.'

'But why do you want to expand?' asked Lucille.

'Because I'm interested. There are other reasons too, but they're what you could call private.'

A woman, perhaps—pushing him into an ambitious programme, wanting more and more money? Lucille couldn't stop the thought racing round her brain, and she also recalled the woman he had met in Amsterdam.

Blair asked her again what she would like to do for the rest of the day.

'I don't know.' She really didn't feel like going sightseeing.

'Perhaps you should rest,' he told her. 'I have one or two people to see this afternoon, then this evening I suggest we avail ourselves of their room service and have dinner up here. What do you say?'

'Dinner up here?' she echoed. Somehow the idea of an intimate dinner party for two aroused a confusion of thoughts in her mind from which she shrank. 'To—to test the service, I suppose you mean?'

'Of course. Now I suggest you have a rest, then ring down for some tea or whatever you want. In fact, some tea would be a good idea—see if they make it the English way.'

He disappeared into the bathroom, then a few minutes later went out, leaving her feeling somewhat limp and in a degree of mental disarray. What on earth had she let herself in for with this job? she asked herself. Here she was, sharing a suite of rooms with a man she hardly knew, allowing herself to be persuaded against her better judgement, and reacting emotionally in a way she simply could not understand. How could she possibly allow Blair to take up his mattress and sleep in the dressing-room as he had suggested? It was ridiculous. What would the maids think? Yet she shrank from the idea of his occupying the other bed, only a few feet away. She had never done such a thing even with Jim.

At the thought of Jim her conscience smote her. She had sent him one postcard since leaving London, that was all. She really must get in touch with him. It was past three o'clock—they had taken an age over lunch.

He would be at Reception, and this was not a very busy hour. She would ring him right now.

She picked up the bedside telephone and asked to be given the number. Within a remarkably short space of time she heard Jim's voice answering the ring in exactly the same way she had answered it herself hundreds of times, terminating in, 'Can I help you?'

She had not realised how wonderful it would be to hear his voice again.

'Jim, it's me—Lucille.'

There was a moment's silence, then delight and relief was evident in his voice as he replied.

'Lucille—thank goodness! I've been wondering what's happened to you. Where are you?'

'In Paris.'

'Paris? But why didn't you let me know where you were going? I want to keep track of you so that I know where you are. I might want to come and see you. Where are you staying?'

She told him the name of the hotel. 'But, Jim, we shall only be here a short time, and——'

He interrupted her. 'Lucille, I have to go. Quick, give me the number of your hotel and I'll ring you back later.'

She did so, then they both rang off. Lucille sighed. It was going to be difficult for Jim to keep track of her movements as they didn't appear to be staying in one place more than a few days. And so far, Blair had not informed her of their itinerary. She would have to ask him. Feeling suddenly weary, she kicked off her shoes and flung back the bedcover. What with the journey and the heavy lunch she felt she would fall asleep any minute. She pulled off her skirt and blouse and slid under the bedcover in her slip. As she closed her eyes, she thought vaguely of the unpacking she had not done. But there would be plenty of time before Blair returned.

The next moment she was jolted awake by the feel of a weight on the bed, and opened startled eyes to see Blair sitting there, arms folded as though he'd been sitting there for hours and an odd expression on his face, his eyes flickering over her bare arms and shoulders which showed over the top of the bedcover.

In an instinctive gesture she knew would look silly and prudish, she pulled the cover over arms and shoulders.

He eyed her in silence for a moment, then he commented, 'I have seen bare arms and shoulders before, you know. Have you had tea?'

'Why, no, I——' Lucille glanced at her watch. 'Good heavens, six o'clock! It'll be too late now.'

'In a hotel like this it's never too late—or too early—to get anything you want, except for a five-pound note out of the till. If you want tea, ring for it. I could do with a cup, anyway. And dinner is any time we want it—within reason.'

'Yes. Yes, of course.'

She had already uncovered her left arm to look at her watch. Now Blair watched with a cynical smile as she brought her right hand and arm to pick up the telephone. She hoped he wasn't going to sit there looking at her when she wanted to emerge to get a wrap. Walking around in her underwear while he was around would be creating an intimacy she did not wish for.

She asked for tea for two to be sent up and put down the phone, but Blair still sat there, like a theatregoer waiting for the curtain to rise.

She sighed. 'Blair, do you mind going into the sitting-room, please. I want to get off the bed and unpack my case. Yours too.'

He shook his head. 'I've never met such a puritan in all my life! What's the matter? Got a ladder in your stocking?' he mocked.

'Please——' she begged.

With a look she couldn't begin to interpret he stood up, turned and went into the other room. Her heart pounding for no accountable reason, Lucille swung

her legs to the floor and hastily pulled on her skirt and
blouse again. So he thought her a puritan, did he? Her
mind raced. All right, perhaps she was, but that was
better than being promiscuous. She opened her suitcase
and began to unpack, feeling a mixture of emotions.
Somewhere inside her there was pain and a longing for
she knew not what. She was hurt by some of the things
Blair was saying to her, disturbed by his presence, un-
certain as to what was going on in his mind at times.
He was supposed to be her employer, but much of the
time she couldn't feel that he was. Sharing this suite with
him—it was all wrong, and it was not all to do with
propriety. Then what? she asked herself. It was because
she was finding that close proximity to him was beginning to have a strange effect on her. She longed for
him to touch her, but knew that if he did——

He called out to her that the tea had arrived, and she
braced herself to join him. He was sitting on the elegant
settee, and she chose deliberately to sit in one of the
armchairs.

'Do we—er—dress for dinner this evening?' she asked
as he poured the tea.

'Of course,' he answered. 'Must keep up appearances, you know—for the sake of the servants. Or, in
this case, the waiters. Unless, of course,' he added,
'you'd like to dine in your négligé, with me in my—er—
dressing gown.'

She gave him a barbed look. 'Are you being funny or
simply sarcastic?'

He shrugged aggravatingly. 'Take your choice.'

'What choice? You know perfectly well what my
question meant. Of course I'll dress for dinner, if you
wish, and I do wish you'd stop treating me as an employer one minute and—and—something else the next.'

'Something else? Now what on earth do you mean by
that, I wonder?'

Lucille sighed. 'I think you know what I mean.'

He made no answer but continued to regard her with a half calculating, half amused look. Lucille could not quite make him out. At times he seemed to be goading her—or was he testing her? She couldn't be sure. Desperate to change the topic of conversation and stop her brain going round in circles, she began to talk of the time she had spent in Paris when she had been learning the French language.

Then came the inevitable moment when it was time to dress. Lucille wondered whether Blair had taken this kind of thing into account when he arranged for them to share the suite.

'Would you like to use the bathroom first, or shall I?' she felt forced to ask as he failed to do so and the evening was wearing on.

'Oh, ladies first,' he said carelessly.

'Very well.'

Calculating that she would have to dress quickly while he was either having a bath or shower, she first of all laid out all her evening clothes on the bed. She had noticed two clean bathrobes hanging up in the bathroom, so she would rely on that for cover-up as Blair passed through the bedroom. And while he was dressing she could go through into the sitting-room.

Having settled that to her satisfaction, she locked the bathroom door behind her, undressed in there while waiting for the water to run, and emerged some fifteen minutes later, safely wrapped around in the white bathrobe.

'I'm through!' she called out to Blair.

He took his time coming through to the bedroom, and when he did, he looked Lucille up and down in a way that made her feel naked.

'I—hung your clothes in the wardrobe,' she told him, turning away swiftly.

Out of the corner of her eye she saw him take out his dressing gown, but that was all.

'I'll use the dressing-room,' he told her.

Lucille received this piece of information with much relief. She had noticed that the dressing-room contained a dressing-table with mirror and a rack for clothes complete with coathangers.

As soon as she heard splashing in the bathroom, she dressed quickly. She would have to put on her make-up last. She was struggling to zip up her dress when Blair emerged wearing the other bathrobe, which reached only to his knees. Her heart almost stopped beating when he crossed over to her.

'Allow me,' he said, taking her hands away from the zip.

It was the kind of dress that was held up by two straps, under which she wore only a waist slip and no bra. As his fingers ran up her spine with the zip, a peculiar feeling touched her. It was not a cheap sexual thrill; it went deeper than that. It was as though the whole universe had temporarily stopped. His fingers lingered at the top of the dress, and she wanted them to stay there for ever. With an effort she pulled herself to the surface, and was about to thank him and move away from him when he swung her round to face him, his hands on her bare shoulders.

He eyed her cynically. 'I thought you didn't like showing your bare shoulders? An hour or so ago you tried to cover them up.'

Lucille gathered herself together. All her instincts were to move closer to him, but she knew she must resist.

She twisted away from him. 'That was different. I'm dressed now. Then, I was only half dressed.'

'Oh yes, of course,' he said sarcastically.

Lucille wondered how much more of this she could take. He smelled strongly of wholesomeness and aftershave, his dark hair slightly damp and the half-open towel robe showing virile hairs on his chest.

With a mocking smile he moved away from her and went through into the dressing room.

Lucille gave a large sigh and sat down on the bed, her legs shaking. She was becoming attracted to Blair Saunders, that's what was happening. And it must stop. He was playing some kind of game with her, amusing himself, enjoying seeing her embarrassed and discomfited. She must show him she didn't care, call his bluff, be on her dignity—anything. But this was definitely the last time she would share an apartment or anything else with him.

She applied her make-up and fastened a piece of jewellery around her neck that Jim had once bought her. She was sure it had not been expensive, knowing what Jim's salary was, but it was just right for this dress and even *looked* expensive. Finally she draped a lacy stole around her shoulders. Blair seemed to find them an object of scrutiny, so she would not give him that pleasure.

She went through to the sitting-room. Blair had earlier ordered a selection of drinks in addition to those already in the small refrigerated cocktail cabinet, and she thought it would be a good idea to pour out a couple.

'What would you like to drink?' she called out to him.

There was a momentary silence, then he answered, 'You should know by now.'

Lucille felt she just couldn't win. She tried to think, then remembered that he drank neat whisky as an aperitif. She gave a wry smile. A man's drink, for sure! She found the right glass and poured him a generous measure, then helped herself to a glass of sherry. Whisky was not for her.

Blair emerged shortly looking even more handsome and distinguished than before. She had placed his drink on the small table at one end of the settee where he had sat for tea, but before he took his seat, he picked up the continental telephone on a table beside the wall and rang to ask for dinner menus to be sent up.

'Ah,' he said, eyeing his drink. 'So you remembered.'

She nodded. 'As a good secretary should.'

He sipped his drink appreciatively. 'I can never understand,' he said, holding his glass up to the light, 'why some men order whisky, then water it down, whether with the stuff from the tap, soda, ginger ale or anything else.'

Intolerance of the first order, she thought. 'Surely it's a matter of personal taste,' she commented.

'Mm,' he murmured, sipping again. 'Like one's taste in women.'

'I take it you like women who are—undiluted.' It was the only word she could think of which fitted. 'Strong' wouldn't have sounded right.

He nodded approvingly. 'That's a very good word. Undiluted, distinctive, mature, and altogether pleasing to the senses.'

As he was speaking Lucille tried to visualise the kind of woman he liked and, presumably, would marry. He had said nothing about beauty. But then that would hardly have been applicable to whisky.

'Spirit, perhaps?' she offered. 'As that's what you're drinking.'

He inclined his head. 'That too.' His glance shifted to her own modest glass of sherry. 'And what about you? Tell me what kind of man appeals to you.'

She shrugged. 'I don't know. I just don't think about it. But if we're equating drinks with the sexes——' she picked up her glass and held it up to the light, 'this is a full-flavoured, matured sherry, not too dry, not too sweet, and yet not quite medium. At least, not the stuff that often passes for medium. Full-blooded, plenty of body,' she added without thinking, or at least, thinking of the sherry.

But Blair was not simply thinking of sherry. 'Full-blooded and plenty of body? So that's how you like your men, is it?'

She stared at him, praying that her cheeks would not colour as she realised what she had said.

'I was referring to sherry,' she answered with a coolness she did not feel.

'Really? I thought we were "equating drinks with the sexes",' he reminded her.

Lucille was greatly relieved when a knock came on the door and a waiter came in with the menus.

'Shall I wait, sir?' he asked, producing his notepad.

'No, no. Come up again in about five minutes' time,' Blair told the man.

He went out. Lucille hoped Blair would not reopen the subject of what kind of man she preferred. But he had one more thing to say.

'I think that's the kind of man you'd want too,' he agreed. 'I can't see you settling for a weakling. But tell me, what are the main criteria by which you would choose a husband?'

She wanted to say to him, Please couldn't we talk about the hotel business, discuss the menu, anything but these personal subjects? She couldn't think what had come over him. Still, she answered him as best she could.

'But one doesn't just *choose* a life partner. Surely a man doesn't, either? It's not like buying a piece of furniture—or even a hotel,' she added pointedly.

'Point taken. But do go on.'

'Well—surely one simply falls in love.'

'Just like that?'

'Not on sight, perhaps, in fact I dare say sometimes the opposite happens. But you fall in love because you like the way a person talks, for their ideas, their character, their—their——'

'Charisma?' Blair offered.

'Er—yes, whatever that may mean.' She knew, of course, what he meant. It was that certain something which attracts one man to a woman above all others, and one woman to a man, no matter how many others they might meet. But she had no wish to keep up this conversation. 'Please, can we order dinner?' she pleaded. 'I'm starving!'

'Certainly,' he said, giving her a calculating look before handing one of the menus to her.

The waiter returned, and there was the usual lengthy discussion about each item, then the choosing of the wine, and a short time later there arrived two waiters with two trolleys. With great aplomb one trolley was transformed into a table and set with deft speed. The other held the first course, and while one waiter served them, the other disappeared with one of the trolleys, presumably to bring up the main course. No wonder staying in a hotel like this costs money, thought Lucille. A meal here, served privately, would keep an average family for a week!

After a delicious meal of lobster soup, whitebait with a wonderful sauce, roast duckling *à l'orange*, the most succulent *petits pois* Lucille had ever tasted and a dessert out of this world, Blair dismissed the waiter and said he would pour the champagne himself. Lucille was beginning to feel what she could only describe as mellow when suddenly the telephone rang.

'Damn and blast. Who can that be, I wonder?' muttered Blair rather savagely. 'I gave strict instructions that I didn't want to be disturbed.' Lucille half rose to answer it, but he motioned to her to stay where she was, finishing her dessert.

'Yes, hello,' he said brusquely. 'Who is it? *Who?* Who the devil—— I see. Hold on a minute.'

He turned and looked at Lucille coldly. 'It's for you. Somebody called Jim.'

CHAPTER SIX

LUCILLE got to her feet, feeling literally that her heart had gone down to her boots. Blair was obviously annoyed at the interruption in their evening. It had not occurred to her that Jim would ring at this time—yet it should have. When she had spoken to him in the afternoon, there had been very little time in which to tell him anything, of course.

She picked up the receiver and said, 'Hello, Jim.'

Almost before she had got the words out of her mouth, Jim demanded, 'Who in the world was that who answered the phone.'

'Mr Saunders,' she answered, her heart flopping down still further.

'Your boss, you mean?' came Jim's voice incredulously. 'What on earth is *he* doing in your room?'

What on earth could she say? She couldn't possibly tell him the truth. He wouldn't understand, and she could hardly blame him.

'We're—having dinner,' she told him lamely. 'It's to—to test the room service.'

'I see,' he said in a tone which implied that he didn't 'see' at all. 'And how long will you be there—at that hotel?'

'Only a couple of days—I think.'

'You think!' he repeated. 'And where are you going next, may I ask?'

'You may ask, but I don't know.' Lucille was beginning to feel faintly annoyed at his tone. 'I'll give you a ring when we get there.'

'And by that time—if you're only staying a few days at a time in one place—it'll be too late for me to come out to you, anyway.'

'I'm sorry, but I can't help that. And I really must ring off now.'

'But, Lucille, you know I don't trust that man. I told you before you went——'

'Goodbye, Jim,' she said firmly, and replaced the receiver.

She turned back to Blair. 'The champagne is nice and cold,' he said in an offhand voice.

She could sense his displeasure, but dragged up her sagging heart, determined that she was not going to allow him to dictate to her beyond the bounds of employer, or to allow him to bully her.

He handed her a glass of champagne. 'How did he know you were here?' he asked in a cold, quiet voice.

'I rang him this afternoon,' she answered, a note of defiance in her voice.

'With what object, may I ask?'

May I ask. Lucille was getting a little tired of the phrase. 'Yes, you may ask—and I'll tell you. I rang because he's a friend of mine.'

She waited for what he would say next. Surely he wouldn't try to make any objections to her telephoning a friend? If he did she would——

'Is that all?' he questioned.

'What do you mean—*is that all*?' Lucille genuinely didn't know whether he was referring to her relationship with Jim or whether he was trying to probe further into her motive for ringing him.

'I mean,' he answered, 'is he going to come flying over here to see you?'

'He didn't say,' she flung back at him heatedly. 'And even if he were——'

His jaw became taut, his eyes glittered dangerously. 'Do I have to repeat all over again that I want no distractions on this enterprise?'

But Lucille was in no mood to be cowed. 'It's still a free country. If Jim—or anyone else, for that matter—wants to fly over to Paris or any part of Europe, then he's perfectly free to do so,' she retorted, adding, for good measure, 'And there's nothing you can do about it.'

He pointed a long finger at her, looking more angry than she had ever seen him. 'Let me remind you that you entered into a contract with me, a contract for six months' uninterrupted, concentrated work—and that meant no boyfriends hanging around, distracting you, wasting your time.'

He was right, she knew this at heart, but he was not going to win so easily, she thought wildly.

'All right! But at least you could let me know in advance where we're going, so that my friends know where I am and where to get in touch with me in—in case of emergency or——'

'What emergency? Don't worry, there won't be any emergencies that I don't know about, and Ferrari knows our whereabouts—which,' added Blair, giving her a barbed look, 'he has strict instructions not to give to anyone.'

Lucille put down her glass. She felt one more sip of the expensive champagne would choke her. She had never known anyone so unpredictable, so dictatorial in her whole life! She rose to her feet, feeling that enough was enough. Without a word she went into the bedroom and took her suitcase from the wardrobe. There was no law which could keep her here for a moment longer. All the money in the world would not make her go on with this trip. She began to take her clothes from their hangers.

'And what do you think you're doing?' came his voice from the doorway.

'What does it look as though I'm doing?' she answered recklessly.

'It looks as though you're packing, of course,' he answered smoothly. 'Let me put it another way. Why are you packing tonight—at this minute—and where is your destination?'

'London is my destination,' she told him. 'I'm going home.'

'You're doing nothing of the kind!'

She swung round furiously. 'I'm going, and you can't stop me!'

'Oh yes, I can—and I will. By force, if necessary.'

'You wouldn't dare!' she answered, her eyes blazing.

'Oh yes, I would. As you said earlier, you don't know me. Now, put those clothes back in the wardrobe and come and finish your drink.'

For answer, Lucille folded the dress lying on the bed and put it in her case.

Blair strode angrily across the room, took hold of her and flung her across to the other bed, then he picked up her case and emptied the contents in a heap. She stared at him wide-eyed. This man was not only dictatorial, he was a brute. He *could* force her by physical means to stay. The only way she was going to escape him was by giving him the slip some time tomorrow and hiring a taxi to take her to Orly Airport. She watched him as he strode to the wardrobe and put back her case. He was a very determined man. The only thing she could do was pretend to give in, to hang up her clothes again and let him think he had won. She stood up and began to pick up her clothes. He then stood and watched her while she hung them up again.

'That's better,' he said when she had finished. 'And don't let us have any more of that kind of nonsense.'

If she'd had anything to hand she would have thrown it at him. As it was, she gritted her teeth and followed him back into the sitting-room. She sipped her drink, and in spite of the way she was feeling, began to enjoy it.

'Have some more,' Blair said as she emptied her glass.

'Well—just one more.'

He seated himself opposite her and gave her a long, calculating look. Then he said suddenly, 'That's a very beautiful dress you're wearing. Did you buy it specially for this trip?'

Lucille was beginning to feel relaxed. The effect of the champagne, she supposed.

'Yes, I did, as a matter of fact. I'm—glad you like it.' She was inwardly staggered to hear herself say such a thing, and be sincere about it. Yet five minutes ago they had almost come to blows. They were behaving more like—like a couple of lovers or husband and wife than anything else. Oh, my goodness, she thought wildly. What on earth is happening to me? It's this darned champagne!

'You're fond of nice clothes, aren't you?' It was more of a statement than a question.

It was true, but she didn't want him to get a wrong impression of her. 'Not abnormally so, but if you're wearing something you like, something good and suitable for the occasion, it gives you confidence.'

His brows lifted slightly. 'I shouldn't think you need a thing like clothes to give you confidence. It seems to me you've got *plenty* of that.'

She wasn't sure whether this was meant as a compliment or not. 'In what way do you think I've got plenty of confidence?' she asked him.

He pursed his lips in what was almost a smile. 'Well— the way you stand up to me, for example.'

'I only do that when I feel I have to,' she flashed back.

'Really? But it's not just that, of course. It's your whole demeanour.'

'I've simply become accustomed to meeting people, that's all,' she answered. 'But please, can we talk about something else?'

'Yes. Have some more champagne,' he said at once, and withdrew the bottle from its ice bucket.

'No, no, I mustn't,' she protested.

'Oh, come on. It would be a pity to waste it, and I can't drink it all myself. Besides, if we drink an equal amount, we shall be equally—er—tipsy, or pleasantly hazy, whichever way you like to put it.'

Was it her imagination, or had his voice taken on a different note—persuasive, cajoling? Lucille found herself quite unable to keep up with his moods.

She capitulated. 'Yes, all right. Just one more, then I really must go to—to bed.'

Somewhere at the back of her mind lurked the thought that 'going to bed' was not going to be the simple act that it sounded. Unless Blair moved his mattress and bedding all into the dressing-room, his bed would be only a few feet away from her own.

She watched him as he went back to his own chair and poured out the last of the champagne for himself. He was a very attractive man, she thought, and over the rim of her glass she studied his face. There was a decided strength to his mouth and jaw, his hair was well cut, dark and abundant, his nose straight, his lips—— She found herself concentrating on his lips and wondering what it would be like to be kissed by him. Gentle, passionate—— She shivered suddenly and almost spilt her drink. She had been a fool to have this third glass— or was it the fourth? She was even beginning to want him to come across and sit beside her.

'Oh, my goodness!' she exclaimed aloud.

Blair glanced at her swiftly. 'What's the matter?'

She shook her head. 'N-nothing, really. It's—just that I think I've drunk too much of this stuff.'

'Stuff? What a description of such a vintage! Don't worry. It can be heady, I know, but it will soon wear off—and you'll sleep like a log.'

She couldn't help thinking that *he* certainly seemed to be in full possession of his senses. Maybe he was well accustomed to drinking vintage champagne. Compared with what Jim bought on odd occasions—— But there *was* no comparison, unless one compared nectar with fizzy lemonade.

With every fresh sip of the deliciously cool champagne, Lucille felt more and more lightheaded and carefree. Blair had become remarkably silent, and she wondered vaguely what he was thinking. She felt she ought to start up some topic of conversation, but every time she tried to think, ideas eluded her. She was aware only of a feeling of floating happily and of Blair's face coming and going. She was unaware of the passage of time.

'Lucille——' his voice wafted towards her, 'you look ready for bed. It *is* getting rather late.'

She took another sip—or tried to—but her glass was empty.

'Yes, of course,' she answered, and stood up. But the next minute she found herself sitting down again as the room gave a sideways tilt.

'Let me help you,' he said, coming close to her and putting his hands under her arms.

She froze. 'No, no, I can manage.'

She tried again, and this time managed to stand on her feet, but as soon as she started to walk to the bedroom door she found she couldn't walk straight. Her knees felt weak and she almost sank to the floor. *I'm drunk,* she thought. *I'm drunk. Something I've never been before.*

She must have said it out loud, because she heard Blair say as he put his arm around her, 'You're not drunk, just a little dizzy, that's all.'

Lucille felt distinctly annoyed with herself, and a dozen different warning flashes ran through her brain. She felt almost helpless. Could she trust this man? Jim had warned her. Suppose he——

'Thank you—I'm fine now,' she told Blair as she sank helplessly on to the bed.

'Are you sure?' he persisted. She nodded. 'Well,' he said, 'at least let me unzip you.'

Before she could protest, she felt his fingers once more running down her spine. She held her breath, acutely aware of his nearness and his touch. The dress unzipped, he stood looking down at her for a moment. Then he said, 'Would you really like me to sleep in the other room?'

She glanced across to the other bed, and visualised him dragging off the bedclothes and the mattress. The settee in the sitting-room was certainly not long enough for anyone to sleep on, and even the mattress on the floor would not be very comfortable. She couldn't let him do it. She would have to trust him.

She shook her head swiftly. 'No, no, you'll be most uncomfortable. I don't mind,' she told him.

She was thankful that he left the room so that she was able to undress. Her head was now clearing a little, though it was with a little difficulty that she made her way to the bathroom. How stupid she had been to drink all that champagne! She would never, ever allow herself to get into such a state again. Not trusting herself to get in the bath, or even under the shower, she washed her hands and face and brushed her teeth, then, after making sure that Blair was not in the room, staggered to her bed and slipped between the sheets. She heard the door of the other room open, and the subdued voice of the waiter, who had apparently been asked to come and clear away the dinner trolley, then there was a silence.

Lucille turned on her side away from the other bed and closed her eyes. What was he doing? How long would it be before he came to bed? She stiffened at the thought and wished fervently that she had not let him talk her into this situation. She was in a haze of sleepiness, but she knew perfectly well she would not be able to sleep until both lights were out.

She heard Blair come through the bedroom to the bathroom, then came the sound of running water and splashing, and again a silence. She lay rigid, her eyes closed, her ears straining to catch the slightest sound. The bathroom door opened and she heard the soft pad of his feet as he emerged and crossed the room. She sensed him near her bed and held her breath. If he as much as touched her, she would scream. But surely he wouldn't dare, she thought. Yet she knew that this man would dare anything. She felt his breath faintly on her face and a slight disturbance of the bedclothes, and waited, feeling every nerve taut. With a tremendous effort she lay perfectly still, then she was aware that he had moved, and a few minutes later the room was in darkness.

Very slowly Lucille unwound, and after a minute or two, when she thought she could detect his deep breathing, she turned over on to her back and gave a sideways glance across to the other bed. As her eyes grew accustomed to the darkness she could see the faint outline of his form.

Blair. His name floated around her brain. If only— Suppose he *had* touched her, tried to kiss her or anything? Would she really have screamed? she asked herself. Suddenly she felt she wanted to cry. What on earth was wrong with her? It slowly dawned upon her that she was actually disappointed that he had left her alone. This was dreadful. She tried to dismiss such thoughts, thoroughly despising herself, but it was a long time before she actually went to sleep, in spite of the champagne.

To her surprise, when she awakened the following morning Blair was already dressed and was sitting out on the balcony. What had awakened her was the sound of a knock at the door and a chambermaid bringing in morning tea. Blair instructed the girl to put it on a table on the balcony, then came through and stood in the doorway of the bedroom.

'Sleep well?' he enquired.

Lucille nodded. 'Yes, thank you. And you?'

'Like a top. Come on to the balcony and have some tea. It's lovely and warm. Just put something on, don't stop to get dressed. I shan't eat you!'

Lucille was past feeling coy or shy with him. She put on her négligé, which was not one of the flimsy, see-through kind, brushed her hair and went out to join him.

It was a beautiful morning, warm and still. Blair was obviously waiting for her to pour the tea, so she did. For what seemed a long time neither of them spoke but sipped their tea and gazed out across the lush green of the park. Then Blair turned and gave her one of his top-to-toe scrutinies. But she was becoming accustomed to his stares.

'Well?' she challenged him.

'Very well,' he answered enigmatically. 'Is there any more tea?'

'Of course.' She poured it, then asked him a question. 'And what are we going to do today?'

'What would you like to do?' he countered.

'Anything *you* say.'

'Mm. Well, we'll have to think,' he said lazily, and looked as though he was going to be content to sit there for a very long time.

Lucille frowned and put her hand to her head. She didn't exactly have a hangover, but so much had happened the previous evening, she had forgotten until now her determination to escape him, make her way to the airport and fly back to London.

'Something on your mind?' he asked.

You don't miss a thing, do you? she almost flung back at him. But she kept it to herself. 'I think there's one thing I'd like to do,' she told him.

'And what's that?'

'Go for a nice long, leisurely walk around the park.'

'Good. I'll come with you,' he said promptly.

She was about to protest that she would prefer to go alone, but he was so discerning, he might become suspicious, especially after she had tried to pack last night. Good heavens, she thought, it's worse than trying to escape from a jailer!

After breakfast they went for a walk, then had coffee in one of the many cafés along the Champs-Elysées. Once or twice Lucille was tempted to make a dash for it when an unoccupied taxi drove past. She was reasonably sure that Blair would not make a public scene by trying to restrain her. But a glance at his face, and she was *not* so sure. Perhaps she could slip out of the hotel this afternoon, jump into a taxi and get away. She would no doubt have to leave her luggage behind.

Whether he guessed what was in her mind or not, Lucille had no way of knowing, but he did not let her out of his sight for the rest of the day. After lunch he took her for a trip on the Seine, and there was certainly no chance of grabbing a taxi there. Then after tea on the balcony of their suite he announced that he was taking her to a nightclub.

'Rest for a while if you want to,' he said. 'We shall be late, I've no doubt. I might even have a nap myself. I certainly won't go out.'

Lucille's senses alerted. 'Oh, I don't think I want to rest,' she said casually. 'I think I might take a walk, perhaps look at some of the shops.'

'I wouldn't, if I were you,' he said swiftly. 'We can go in the morning. I don't feel like going out again now—there won't be much time, anyway, before we'll need to dress to go out. And after what happened our first night here I simply can't allow you to go out on your own.'

'But—but this is the better quarter, and it's broad daylight.'

'It makes no difference, Lucille. Now, please—stop arguing and relax for an hour or thereabouts.'

Lucille gave an inward sigh and went through to the bedroom and kicked off her shoes. She might just as well abandon her idea of giving him the slip and catching a plane to London. She was beginning to suspect that he knew what was in her mind. She could have got a taxi to the shopping area, and who would molest her in a busy thoroughfare in broad daylight with lots of people around? Yes, that hadn't occurred to her—to say she would take a taxi there and back to the Rue de Rivoli or the Rue du Faubourg-Saint-Honoré. She reached for her shoes again, then halted. Blair would only find other arguments, or insist on going with her. Besides, if she were honest with herself, she had to admit that she was losing her enthusiasm for the idea of running out on this job. True, Blair Saunders was proving more difficult than she would ever have expected, and she was not sure that she could trust him in other directions either, but on the whole, she mused, she was beginning to enjoy even their rows. Yes, she decided, she would stick it out. And on that thought she replaced her dress with her dressing gown and stretched out on the bed.

She was awakened by the sound of Blair in the shower, and glanced at her watch to find that she had slept for over an hour. She struggled to her feet, still feeling a little hazy, and with a great yawn crossed to the wardrobe, wondering what best to wear. What kind of nightclub did he have in mind? Did one dress up or down? Her only other evening dress had sleeves and was calf-length.

She was still cogitating when Blair came through, clad in his bathrobe.

'Had a good sleep?' he asked.

Lucille nodded. 'I think I've slept too long. Why didn't you waken me?'

His eyebrows raised slightly. 'And have you start screaming?'

She ignored that. 'What sort of place are we going to? I was wondering what to wear.'

'Wear the dress you wore last night,' he said promptly. 'I take it you have a wrap or stole or something?'

She had a white lacy stole, also an evening jacket in silver lamé, either of which would look well with the turquoise dress she had worn last night. It depended on the kind of place they were going to—and he still hadn't told her that. She brought both garments out of the wardrobe as well as the dress, and laid them out on the bed.

'Which do you think?' she asked.

He promptly chose the silver lamé, from which she deduced that they must be going somewhere special.

'Maxim's?' she asked.

'That's right, then on to the Moulin Rouge or the Folies Bergère, according to the way you feel. Ever been to any of them?'

She shook her head. 'Maxim's was way out of my price range. And the other places——' She broke off. She had been going to say that they were not in her line, but changed her mind. 'The same applies to the Moulin Rouge and the Folies Bergère, I suppose.'

'Sure it wasn't the nudes you objected to?' he said, a note of sarcasm in his voice.

'Of course not,' she denied. She was not going to allow him to call her a prude again. She had once been prevailed upon to go to a nightclub called the Crazy Horse because the lighting effects were so artistic, but she had found the postures of the nude dancers far from artistic.

Maxim's was another matter. This famous restaurant on the Rue Royale was frequented only by the very rich and famous. She might have known Blair would go there.

But first, as he had said, to dine at Maxim's, and Lucille found it even more sumptuous than she could possibly have imagined. Huge, gilt-framed mirrors lined the walls topped with great golden florets and bows. The lighting and the general atmosphere was almost awe-inspiring. Lucille tried to look as though she were well accustomed to such a place as Blair put his hand under her elbow. She had heard that if the head waiter of Maxim's recognised you, then you were a person of some importance, so she supposed she shouldn't have been surprised when Blair was immediately recognised and greeted by name. The fact did make her wonder, however, how often he had been here in the past, and with what woman. A table had obviously been reserved for them—one with its back to the wall enabling them to sit side by side, and not so near the orchestra, so that conversation could be carried on without raising one's voice.

Here the food was more important than the cabaret. Lucille could scarcely believe that she was sitting here. The long discussion about the menu, the merits—there were no demerits—of each item, what they contained, how they were cooked, what wine went with what went, for the most part, over her head. So did the seemingly endless procession of waiters, bringing this, taking away that. But the food was superb.

'Well?' quizzed Blair. 'Are you enjoying the food and everything?'

'Of course,' she answered. 'Who wouldn't?'

'Precisely. So you have no objection to having a taste of the luxury that my kind of money can buy.'

'Only because you've invited me here and that you're my employer. One meal here would keep an ordinary family for a whole week!'

'Yes, I'm afraid so. So you see, in spite of the French Revolution there are still the rich and the poor—though not quite in such extremes.'

Lucille could have argued with him further on the subject of the rich and the poor, but she felt this was hardly the atmosphere for a fierce political debate. Besides, she was too aware of Blair as a man.

'I noticed that the head waiter knew you,' she said, 'and that you've been given one of the best tables. You must have been here many times before.'

'A few,' he admitted. 'But it's more than on the basis of recognising my face that he knew me. I'm well known as a hotelier and these things get around in the trade, as you might say.'

'You're—you're not thinking of buying Maxim's, are you?'

He threw back his head and laughed. 'It has crossed my mind, but Maxim's has more than one "owner".'

Before the meal was even half over Lucille found a feeling of well-being taking possession of her. At the present moment there was nothing she wanted more in the world than to be here in this close proximity with Blair. A ridiculous feeling, of course, and one certainly not shared by him, but this registered with her only vaguely. Once or twice she felt the gentle pressure of his thigh on hers, but she did not move away. A strange feeling of a different kind was coursing through her veins. She longed to touch his hand, to feel his arms about her, and as her mind gave full rein to the idea she floated on a cloud of contentment laced with something approaching desire.

At midnight, Blair suggested they might leave. He presented his credit card, left generous tips, and guided Lucille outside where several taxis waited.

'Where now?' she asked him as the commissionaire opened the door for them.

'Where would you like?'

She sank back on to the seat in a daze. 'I don't really know, but I think either the Folies Bergère or the Moulin Rouge would be something of an anticlimax after Maxim's.'

'I agree,' he murmured, and gave the taxi driver the name of their hotel.

The taxi moved off, and suddenly Lucille found herself in Blair's arms, his mouth on hers. Swiftly, her arms went around his neck and her lips trembled under his. She felt one of his hands search beneath her jacket to find her bare shoulders and she almost passed out as his touch ran along her nude flesh. She felt his passion rising and her own responded as he held her ever closer to him and his kisses became more ardent. Then a screech of brakes jolted them into one corner, and Blair swore as the taxi driver narrowly missed a collision with a private car.

Blair released her and remonstrated with the man, and there followed a rapid exchange in French, the driver protesting that it had not been his fault.

'Moi, le frapper? C'est ridicule!'

But they were soon back at the hotel. Blair paid the driver, then helped Lucille out. She had by this time composed herself a little and was now feeling shy of him. She really shouldn't have let her feelings run away with her like that, she told herself. It had been an impulse on his part, that was all. They made their way up to their suite in silence. Lucille wondered what Blair was thinking. Was he regretting having kissed her? The best thing she could do was behave as though it had not happened.

The silence between them still held when they entered their sitting-room. Lucille scarcely knew what to say. It had been a wonderful evening, and though she felt they had been jolted into reality by the near-collision of the taxi, there remained a certain something in the atmosphere.

It was Blair who broke the silence. 'Would you like a drink?'

It was a typical male question in the circumstances. Recalling the previous evening, she shook her head. 'No, thanks. I think I'll go straight to bed, if you don't mind. Thanks for a lovely evening—I did enjoy it.'

It was a gross understatement. He made no reply. Lucille took a swift glance at his face, but could read nothing in his expression. She walked slowly into the bedroom, a mixture of emotions, the feel of his lips still strong, and her shoulders under her jacket still tingling from his touch.

Blair did not even say goodnight. She dropped her evening bag on to the bed and stood there for a moment, then all at once she was aware of him standing behind her. He turned her round to face him, an odd expression on his face. Without a word he slipped her jacket from her shoulders and removed it altogether. She held her breath and shivered a little. Still without speaking, he reached round for the zip of her dress and slowly pulled it down. Her heart began to beat rapidly and she knew she was powerless to resist anything he might do. She wanted to speak his name, but no word would come; all she could do was just stand there.

His hands caressed her bare shoulders, then very slowly he slid the straps of her dress down over her arms until it slid away from her waist and fell down to her ankles.

CHAPTER SEVEN

AFTER a restless night Lucille slept late, and when she looked across at Blair's bed it was empty, the bedclothes flung back carelessly. She listened intently, but could hear no sign.

She closed her eyes against the memory of last night, wishing that she had indeed caught that plane back to London. She had spent half the night weeping silently. She was in love with Blair—she realised that now. She had reached this conclusion during the small hours of the morning. Blair could have done anything he wanted with her, but after letting her dress fall, he had turned away from her and left her, going back into the other room. She had felt like weeping then. She had finished undressing and slipped into bed, expecting, half hoping, wanting Blair to come to her and take her in his arms. But he was so long in returning, she put out her light, and when he came to bed he did not come near her. Her heart cried out to him, was still crying out to him. She loved him. She would never love another man for as long as she lived. But he had said not a word.

She reached for her dressing-gown and went into the other room, expecting to see him sitting on the balcony, but it was empty. She stepped out and looked across the park. Away under a group of trees, she saw him, his hands thrust deep into his pockets. If he had wanted her last night he would have said so. If he had loved her he would surely have said so. Obviously, what he had done was simply a result of having wined and dined well. Now he was regretting it, fearing perhaps that she might make more of it than he had intended. He started back to the hotel, or at least in that direction, and Lucille waved to him, but he did not respond.

She rang for some tea, and while waiting for it to arrive, had a quick shower and slipped on a dress. He must not come back and find her undressed. She must behave as though nothing had happened; he would prefer it that way. But she knew that she would never feel the same again now. She would have to guard her tongue and her every look and gesture, and above all, avoid his touch. In all, re-establish their former employer/employee relationship.

Blair walked into the suite just as she was pouring out a cup of tea, her folder of reports lying on the table. She must appear to be businesslike, she had thought. But the sight of him, fresh from his walk, caused her heart to miss a beat.

'Hello!' she called out with a cheerfulness which sounded artificial even to her own ears. 'You're just in time for some tea. Or do you want breakfast? It's almost ten o'clock.'

She hardly dared even look at him as he joined her on the balcony and sat down.

'A coffee and a roll will do for me later,' he said. 'But you get something to eat for yourself whenever you feel like it. We're moving on after lunch,' he added unexpectedly.

'You mean—going to the next hotel? But—but where?'

'Venice,' he answered briefly as he picked up the cup of tea she had poured for him.

Lucille stared at him. 'Venice—tonight? That's impossible!' She was nettled that he had sprung the decision on her like this. She had somehow thought they would be here for at least one more day, since he had made no mention of leaving Paris last night.

'Venice is the location of our next prospective hotel,' he answered without looking at her. 'We shan't make it tonight, of course. I know several hotels in Lyon. I'll ring them when I've had this tea and make reservations in one of them,' he added in a toneless voice.

She stole a glance at his profile, but his face was devoid of expression too, and his whole attitude was aloof. It had been unnecessary for her to be on her guard against him. He obviously wanted to forget last night. How was she going to bear being with him for the rest of this project, loving him as she did? She ought to tell him now, this minute, that she couldn't go on with it.

But she found herself saying, 'While you're doing that I'd better start packing.'

'Yes,' he answered, and rose to his feet. But at the door leading into the sitting-room he turned, his eyes focusing on the wallet containing her reports. 'Don't bother writing a report on this hotel,' he told her brusquely. 'I'll do it myself.'

Lucille looked after him, a dull ache settling around her heart. She simply would not be able to bear it if he were like this for long. She would rather they were quarrelling. Yet she knew she could not bring herself to leave him, either.

Eyeing her tea with distaste, she left it and went through to the bedroom. Blair was using the telephone in the sitting-room, and it crossed her mind that this would doubtless be the first and the last time that he would book a suite for them. Had he been testing her last night to see how far she would allow him to go? Perhaps he thought she let every man she met practically strip her. The thought depressed her utterly. But what would be the use of trying to tell him that? If she told him she loved him he would be embarrassed. Besides, at the time he had aroused her in the taxi and then she had allowed him to remove her dress, she hadn't known that she did love him.

She heaved a large sigh and set about packing her suitcase. Whatever happened, she must never again allow her emotions to get the better of her. The only way to do that as far as Blair was concerned was to keep a reasonable distance from him. But from his changed attitude this morning he was unlikely to want to touch her, she decided with a heavy heart.

After coffee and rolls about eleven o'clock, they set off for Lyon. Blair drove with fierce concentration, scarcely speaking a word, while Lucille tortured herself wondering what he thought of her. The same questions went round and round in her brain. Why had he begun to make love to her and then stopped? How much of it had meant anything beyond a normal man's passion for a woman with whom he had spent a pleasant evening? Why hadn't she stopped him sooner? Her head began to ache, and she was glad when they stopped for a light and rather late lunch.

'Are you all right?' asked Blair with no real sign of tenderness in his voice as he caught sight of her face across the lunch table.

'I have a slight headache, that's all,' she told him honestly.

'Have you got any aspirin or anything in your bag?'

'I think so.'

'Then take a couple!' he almost flung at her.

Lucille felt like bursting into tears, and as though to stave off such a thing happening, she allowed her anger to rise.

'There's no need to sound so unfeeling!' she flashed back at him.

His eyebrows raised. 'Bad-tempered too, it seems.'

She glared at him. 'A hangover from last night, perhaps,' she said, and immediately could have kicked herself.

For what seemed like an age he made no reply, then, 'The least said about last night the better. Take your aspirins. We have a long drive ahead, and this isn't England where you can get a cup of tea every couple of miles.'

'No, but we might be able to get coffee at a café,' she snapped.

'Coffee at a café,' he repeated. 'Very funny.' But he wasn't smiling.

'It wasn't meant to be funny,' she told him, all her good intentions of maintaining an employer/employee relationship coming to nothing. But she was beyond caring. She had to keep saying something to hide her true feelings. What had he said? The least said about last night the better? Well, he had taken the initiative, not she, and she was not going to forget it in a hurry—though I wish to heaven I could, her thoughts went in a crazy, contradictory fashion.

She finished her cold meat and salad, though she nearly choked over it, then swallowed down a couple of aspirins with the last of her coffee. But she knew it would take more than a couple of headache tablets to cure the pain she was really suffering.

Again, for most of the afternoon Blair drove like the wind and in silence. Lucille was almost at screaming point with the tension when he pulled up at a café. Café for coffee. Coffee for café, her brain repeated. Normally she would have seen the joke, but she was too strung up to see the funny side of anything.

At last, with barely time to change for dinner, they arrived at the hotel in Lyon where—as Lucille had predicted—Blair had booked separate rooms for them which were next door to each other.

'Give me a knock when you're ready to go down,' he told her. 'It's best if we go down at the same time.'

There was not the slightest sign of warmth in his voice, and Lucille felt miserable beyond belief.

She washed her hands and face, renewed her make-up and put on another dress, then braced herself to knock on his door. He came out to join her immediately. He showed very little sign of strain after the day of hard driving, but he certainly seemed to have something on his mind.

Though the hotel was of a good standard, there was not quite the fuss and ceremony over the food that there had been in Paris. They were nearing the end of the main course when a waiter brought a telephone to their table.

'A call for you from England, *monsieur*. Mees Gregory.'

Immediately Blair's face relaxed into a smile as he picked up the receiver.

'Hello—and how's my girl?' he said in a voice full of tenderness. 'Oh, not bad,' he continued in a reply to the woman at the other end. 'We shall be in Venice tomorrow. I'll give you a ring on arrival. You should have come with me, you know. I miss you.' There was a pause. 'Yes, I know. You got my letter and card from Paris? Good. And what are you doing now?' There was a longish silence while apparently the woman at the other end gave him an account of how she was spending her evening. Then, 'Are you trying to make me jealous? Well, just behave yourself until I get back. All right, darling, I will.' He laughed as he replaced the receiver, but there was no doubting the tender expression in his eyes. 'I'm sorry about that,' he said to Lucille, but gave no further explanation as to his caller, and for the rest of the meal it was obvious that his thoughts were elsewhere.

'Would you like to go for a walk?' he asked when they had finished their meal.

She would have loved to have gone out into the warm still night with him and walked the streets of Lyon with her hand in his, but as it was——

'No, I don't think so,' she answered. 'I feel more like an early night.'

'As you wish,' he said with marked indifference, and walked towards the street door while she took the lift upstairs. Afterwards, she began to wish she *had* gone

for a walk, as her mind dwelt on every word of Blair's
telephone call. From his changed expression and the way
he had spoken to the woman at the other end it was
someone who meant a great deal to him. It made his
behaviour towards herself the previous evening even
more puzzling. On top of a tiring day, her head was beginning to ache again, and, feeling the need of something to distract her mind from her agonising thoughts,
she picked up her bedside telephone and asked to be
connected to London, giving the number of Jim's flat.
He would surely be home by now. But, greatly to her
disappointment, there was no reply. Another attempt to
reach him at the hotel was also disappointing. Jim was
not there; he had gone off duty a long time ago.

With a great sigh Lucille replaced the receiver and went
through the procedure of preparing for bed. It was long
past midnight before she heard Blair's key in the lock
of his room.

The next day's journey from Lyon to Venice was much
more interesting, leading as it did through some of the
most beautiful mountain scenery in Switzerland. She had
nothing but admiration for Blair's driving, and she noticed that he seemed much less strained today than yesterday. Not that this gave her a great deal of comfort,
since she related his better mood to his telephone call of
the previous evening. However, he seemed to share her
appreciation of the scenery, and they had an excellent
lunch in Turin with time to have a short walk around
the town. At Verona, they stopped for coffee at a
pavement café overlooking the huge amphitheatre which
resembled in some ways the Colosseum in Rome.

'Have you been to Venice?' he asked her.

'Well, yes, but only on day trips from Lido di Jesolo.
I take it the hotel you're interested in is actually in Venice
itself?'

'Yes, on the Giudecca Canal. Not as long as the Grand
Canal, but wider.'

'But why not a hotel on the Lido?' she asked.

'I don't necessarily want holiday hotels. Many businessmen come to Venice too. In fact—though I know you don't like the idea of making money—it's the businessmen who can afford to pay more for accommodation—and to spend more at the bars. Remember that when you're looking for points for your report.'

Just in time Lucille stopped herself from replying 'Yes, sir'. She made no reply at all, though she had the feeling he had been goading her.

Venice has been called the most beautiful city in the world. To Lucille it was more than that. She found it the most exciting. Formerly she had reached Venice across the lagoon from Punta Sabbioni, but arriving by car they had to cross the three-mile shallow salt lagoon from Mestre by the causeway. Here, in the Piazzale Roma, blue with exhaust fumes and diesel smoke, Blair left the car in the six-storey garage—probably the largest in Italy. As Blair knew no Italian, Lucille came into her own, speaking the language and interpreting for him. At last, their luggage deposited in a water taxi, they set off down the Grand Canal.

It was a fascinating last leg of a journey—under the Ponte degli Scalzi, past a *vaporetto* as it thrashed its way along, past the palaces in their faded pastel colours of green, brown and Venetian red which formed wavering reflections, dodging the gondolas which crossed and re-crossed to draw up at the brilliantly striped mooring poles. It was wonderful. Soon, on the left, they passed the Ca' d'Oro palace, then under the Rialto Bridge, made famous by Shakespeare. Then just short of the Ponte dell'Accademia the launch branched off into a narrower canal where the boatman stopped the engine and moored at the hotel landing stage. A small bridge—one of hundreds in Venice—led from a pleasant campo to the entrance of the hotel, a former palace, Blair informed her. But the front of the palace—or hotel—overlooking the Giudecca Canal was not now used as an entrance and was only a façade, there being nowadays so much motor traffic and shipping vessels.

The upper rooms did, however, overlook the canal, and Lucille discovered that her room, next door to that of Blair, shared the same balcony, gay with flowers. She noted, too, that it would be an easy matter for either of them to gain access to each other's rooms. She pondered this for a little while, but decided it was of little importance. Blair was not likely to come to her room uninvited, and she would certainly not venture into his.

She was just finishing dressing for dinner, however, when she caught a glimpse of him. He was looking down at the passing water traffic, having already changed into a dark lounge suit. She longed to join him, to put her arms around his neck, to kiss him. It seemed to her at this moment the most natural thing in the world. What would he say, what would his reaction be? But his attitude since Paris had decidedly cooled towards her.

She put the finishing touches to her make-up, then stepped out on to the balcony to join him. He turned slowly and gave her a long look, but showed neither approval nor disapproval of the dress she wore with its delicate tracery of flowers on a white background. Keeping her feelings well under control, she went and stood beside him, looking down at the water traffic below, mostly small merchant ships and barges.

'Not as exciting as the Grand Canal, but not so noisy either,' Blair remarked. 'As you probably know, the island of Giudecca was given the name for being the home of so many Jews in the past. And also by writers and artists because it's so peaceful. It has some lovely gardens and literary centres.'

Lucille was only half listening to what he was saying. They were standing so closely they were almost touching, and she longed for him to take her in his arms again.

He half turned towards her. 'I take it you're ready to go down? There's half an hour yet before they start serving dinner, but you'll be interested in the bar—an awful name for what used to be the great hall. But there you are. Er—we might as well go through your room, shall we? I can then compare it with mine, though I dare say they're much the same.'

He followed her into her room, closing the ornate double doors behind him. His presence in the room was almost more than she could bear.

'Is it—the same?' she forced herself to ask.

He looked up at the high ceiling with its decorative plasterwork in blue and gold, the ornate fireplace with a rather faded painting above looking something like a Tintoretto, but probably painted by one of his pupils, and the many paintings which lined the walls in the style of Bellini, Tintoretto, Cavallini and others. The floor was in mosaic, dotted here and there with Persian rugs and, dominating the room, a huge double bed.

'Yes,' Blair said abruptly. 'It's pretty much the same—even to the double bed.'

'Would you—change them for twin beds if you—bought the hotel?'

'Very likely,' he answered. 'Come on, let's go down. There's no point in dallying up here.'

Lucille was surprised at the harsh tone of his voice. How different from when he had been persuading her to share a suite with him! What exactly had he expected of her in Paris? He had taken the initiative towards a different kind of relationship; now he lost no opportunity of indicating how deeply he regretted it. There was a part of her which regretted it too. If Blair had not taken her in his arms in the taxi, rousing her feelings for him, she would probably not have fallen in love with him, she reasoned. Why did men do these things? Why did they start something, then want to withdraw? Why, oh, why had he not kept their relationship on their former employer/employee basis?

Downstairs, she tried to focus her attention on what had been the great hall of the former palace. Giant marble statues flanked each doorway, a frieze of cherubs in various stances ran the whole range of the room, forming a border between wall and ceiling. Lucille doubted whether she could have actually lived with it, impressive though it was.

'You would have done in those days,' Blair told her when she voiced the thought to him. 'The wealthy Venetians were accustomed to this kind of décor, and as works of art these kinds of things have survived. Among the poor it's different. Take our own country. For the most part, our stately homes have become museum pieces. In fact, reverting to Venice, the whole city is now really a museum. In truth, fashions in all art forms change, generally with the dynasties. There was the period of the Stuarts with their extravagances—something like this, really,' he said, gesturing all around with his hand. 'Then came the simplicity—almost severity— of the Georgian period. In the Victorian era came great fussiness and clutter which the Edwardians began to shed. We next had the futuristic phase in which all human beings appeared to have one eye in the centre of their foreheads, great lumps of material with a large hole in the centre which passed for sculpture, coupled with tubular furniture which passed for modern design. Now we seem to be striking something of a happy medium, reviving the best from each era, moving away from the artificial to the natural—as in the case of the latest portrait of Prince Charles—yet maintaining photography as an art form and reviving the art of tapestry work and embroidery—things like that.'

It was the longest Lucille had heard him speak on any subject. But she could have listened to him if he had gone on several times as long.

'I—I had no idea you knew so much about art. I mean, about its history and trends,' she added, recalling how knowledgeable he had been about the art in the Rijksmuseum in Amsterdam.

Blair shrugged off her compliment. 'Once you become interested in a subject, you add to your knowledge of it all the time. Like you with your knowledge and interest in languages.'

'I suppose so.'

They sat in deep leather armchairs for their aperitif before going into the dining-room for their evening meal. Here again the décor was lavish.

'Would you change anything at all?' asked Lucille.

He glanced around the room. 'Possibly not. Of course, I haven't decided yet whether to buy it. Perhaps your report will influence the decision. But I wouldn't let the works of art and all the statuary influence you unduly. *You* wouldn't be "living with it". Neither would the clientele for long, if the food and the accommodation and service are good so that we don't have to make too many changes of staff. People who come to a place like Venice and stay at a hotel like this expect something unusual and grand in the décor. Modern hotels are all so much alike.'

Lucille agreed with him wholeheartedly. 'It's said that wages are so poor in many of the European countries, with more and more holiday hotels reducing their staff— or unable to get staff because of low wages—that they're resorting increasingly to buffet-style meals, which simply means queueing up for food. Would you be prepared to pay more?'

'Certainly,' he said without hesitation, and Lucille could have kissed him.

After dinner—which was adequate, but lacked the flair of French cooking—Blair suggested a walk. Lucille hesitated. She would love to go for a walk, but being with Blair and not being able to touch him was becoming increasingly difficult. Blair was quick to notice her hesitation.

'Venice is another place where women don't go out walking alone after dark. Do you want to go out or don't you?'

'Yes, I do.'

'Then go and get a wrap or coat or something,' he ordered rather than suggested. 'I'll wait for you in the hall.'

Lucille hated being ordered about. She knew a swift reaction, in spite of the fact that she loved him, and almost refused to go with him, but she loved Venice by night, and on her previous visits the last steamer had left for Punta Sabbioni much too early. So she bit back a retort and went to her room to get a jacket—a lovely mohair cardigan she had bought in London with the money Blair had given her.

It was a lovely evening and there was a special magic in the air. Afraid of physical contact with him, Lucille tried to keep a little apart from him, but on crossing the Ponte dell'Accademia she suddenly stumbled. Swiftly his arm came about her in time to prevent her from falling.

'For heaven's sake be careful! All these bridges are rough and a little steep. Are you all right?'

'Yes, I—I'm all right—thank you,' she answered breathlessly, his touch throwing her whole being out of gear. She started forward again and his arm fell from her shoulders.

But he said, 'You'd better take my hand. Come on—and watch where you're putting your feet.' He glanced down at her high-heeled evening shoes. 'No wonder you tripped—wearing those shoes! Why on earth didn't you put some flat-heeled sandals on or another pair of shoes?'

He took hold of her hand, and she simply could not answer him. His touch was sheer heaven and left her bereft of speech.

They spoke very little as they made their way to St Mark's Square across some half dozen bridges in a kind of dog-leg fashion. Lucille felt every nerve tingling, and in a haze of delight stopped reacting against him and began a sort of game within herself. A game in which Blair loved her.

St Mark's Square was a blaze of light. They strolled all around, looking in the shop windows brilliant with jewellery, Lucille pointing first to this piece, then to that. Blair put his hand on her far shoulder and pointed out a set comprising necklace, bracelet and earrings in deep sapphire.

'Gorgeous—but way out of my price range,' she told him with a light laugh.

'What you want is a rich husband,' he said casually. 'That Jim of yours could never afford to buy you anything like that.'

Her dream—her game came to an abrupt end. 'I don't want a rich husband,' she retorted.

'Oh, yes, you do. You have expensive tastes. Don't keep trying to despise money. It's a useful commodity. It can buy you beautiful things, take you to places.'

'Beautiful things needn't cost the earth,' she answered, turning away from the window. 'What would be the good of having jewellery costing thousands of pounds and being afraid to wear it? Very few people know the real thing, anyway. The real stuff is kept locked up in a safe most of the time.'

'Ah, but *you* would know that what you were wearing was the genuine article, and the knowledge would give you extra poise and assurance. And of course, wearing valuable jewellery, you would never go out unaccompanied.'

'A bodyguard?'

'Your husband—or escort—would be your body-guard,' he answered.

'I can't see myself ever needing that kind of escort,' she insisted.

'Nonsense. You'll always need an escort.'

Lucille was about to retort that she went about the streets of London at any hour of the day or night, but his hand was once again on her shoulder as he led her to a shop window displaying all the best and most wonderful examples of Venetian glass.

'Some of the stuff they make nowadays for the tourists is hideous, in my opinion,' he said. 'Clowns, nondescript vases, multi-coloured gondolas and such-like. But these are beautiful.'

And expensive, she thought. But he was right. There were bowls and vases which looked like delicate lace. There was an elegantly shaped pale green vase with white latticework panels and a handle in glittering gold she would have loved to possess. There were animals of all kinds in beautiful colour blends, not garish at all. She had visited the island of Murano on a previous holiday in Venice, so she had some idea of the way some of the articles were made. She had marvelled then at their craft and she marvelled now.

'Maybe we'll come shopping tomorrow,' said Blair. 'I'm sure there's something you'd like. There are even some necklaces. Their patience and skill is beyond belief.'

They walked along the Riva degli Schiavoni and looked out across the lagoon. The multi-coloured lights of the Lido shimmered into a glorious pattern of colour in the dark water, while on the land the string of lights might have been lured from coloured glass on Murano. Close to hand the dark shapes of the gondolas were cradled at their moorings, rocking peacefully. Lucille wanted the moment to last for ever. The feeling of peace was like nothing she had ever experienced in her life. She knew that she would remember and treasure this night for as long as she lived.

After what seemed a very long time Blair touched her shoulder. 'Come on,' he said quietly, 'let's go. You must be getting chilly standing here.'

They walked back the way they had come in almost complete silence, beyond Blair's 'Be careful here', or 'Watch out, it's a bit rough'.

When they arrived back at the hotel, he did not suggest a drink, as she thought he might, but said goodnight abruptly at the door of the lift.

In her room, Lucille did not know whether she felt happy or weepy. It had been a wonderful evening. She could still feel the impression of Blair's hand encircling hers, touching her shoulder, guiding her around the rough places. But she wanted to weep because what she desired was his love, not his kindness, his chivalry as a man. How was she going to endure the coming months? It was worse when he was kind. When he was being brusque and overbearing she could conjure up anger out of her frustrations and hit out at him.

She drew the curtains of the balcony window and saw that his room was still in darkness. Perhaps he had gone out again. She undressed, had her bath, read for a little while, then put out her light and tried to sleep. But somehow she couldn't, and the room felt suddenly stifling. She reached for her négligé and opened the balcony window a fraction. Blair's room was still in darkness; either he had come up and was already asleep or was still out. Lucille drew her flimsy négligé around her against the sudden chill of the night air and stepped outside for a few minutes. At first her eyes focused upon the lights of the island of Giudecca across the stretch of water, then she started as the figure of Blair loomed up beside her.

CHAPTER EIGHT

'YOU KNOW, you shouldn't stand out here clad in almost nothing,' he said in an odd voice. 'You don't know how tempting you look.'

Instinctively, Lucille drew her thin night attire more closely around her. 'I—I came out for some air, that's all. I couldn't sleep.'

'Neither could I.' Blair took a step closer to her, and with the sudden memory of the night in Paris when he all but took off her dress, she panicked. If he touched her, she would not be able to resist him. If he touched her and then left her, she felt she would die.

'No! No—don't come near me!' she stammered in a staccato voice, and fled into her room. She slammed the door after her and stood with her back to it, panting for breath, her heart beating wildly. She was behaving badly, she knew it. It was more than likely that Blair had had no intention of touching her in the way she thought. The truth was, she wanted him to. She wanted him to take her in his arms, to kiss her, even to make love to her. But she was afraid.

With a swift gesture she tugged back the curtains. She would simply have to put up with being stifled. Why hadn't the room got Venetian blinds, which closed but still let in air? She would have thought all windows in Venice would have them. Surely this was where they were invented? Her mind went round and round in a sort of panic. She tried to calm herself, and sat on the edge of the bed for a few minutes. She really was acting in a most lunatic fashion, she told herself. Even at this very moment she was half hoping that Blair would open the door and come in.

'Damn—damn—damn!' she muttered through her teeth.

It was quite a while before she finally drifted into a restless sleep, and as she had forgotten to order morning tea, it was after nine o'clock before she awoke. She dressed quickly and went downstairs, only to find a note on her plate at the table where they had sat for dinner the previous evening. It was from Blair, saying he would be out all morning, and not to expect him back for lunch.

Clearly, she had annoyed him last night. She sighed. This project was proving disastrous. She really would have to stop reacting so strongly whenever Blair touched her or came close to her. Until she panicked out on the balcony, it had been a wonderful evening. How stupid she had been to go out there in her night attire in the first place! How was she going to apologise to him without making matters worse?

After breakfasting on coffee alone, she went upstairs to where the maids were at work and looked into some of the other rooms. She must try to remember that she was here to work. Being able to speak Italian fluently was a great advantage, and before she went out she even managed to cajole the manager into letting her see the kitchen and speak to the chef in charge and his staff. She made a few notes and then went out. This time she did not cross over the Grand Canal, but strolled along to Longhena's great masterpiece in Venice—the church of Santa Maria della Salute. It was the most beautiful church in the whole of Venice, even surpassing, for Lucille, the famous St Mark's. From great steps of white marble rose two huge, impressive domes, and over all a great tower. This was the last great building erected by the Venetians, and plainly they could never hope to better it.

Lucille climbed the steps and entered the church through what resembled a Roman triumphal arch, and for the next hour or so became lost in the simple yet somehow grand interior.

She found it a balm to her troubled mind and spirit to gaze at the many works of art in the chapels and the walls of the Great Sacristy. The high altar, detached in the middle of the Presbytery and covered with a dome, bore a sculpture by Giusto Le Court and depicted the Plague flying away from the Virgin. The church itself had been erected to thank the Virgin for putting an end to the terrible plague that raged in 1630.

There was still half an hour to go before lunch time, and as Lucille had had no breakfast, she felt she must have some lunch, whether or not Blair joined her. So, arriving back at the hotel she took a chair out on to the balcony and began to write her report on the hotel. After a while, hunger smote her again and she glanced at her watch. In a few minutes it would be time to go down. She stood up to go and wash her hands, and as she turned Blair emerged from his room.

'So this is where you are,' he said.

'Have you been looking for me?' she queried.

'Well, I thought I might have seen you in the Square.' He glanced at the wallet in her hand. 'Don't tell me you've been working!'

'Why not? That's what I'm here for, isn't it?' There was an edge to her voice and she knew it. The sudden sight of him had brought back last night's incident with a rush, and she was on the defensive.

'True,' he answered her. 'But I don't want you to stick around the hotel *all* the time.'

'I haven't,' she told him. 'I did some research, then went and had a look at Santa Maria della Salute.' She glanced at her watch again. 'I'm hungry—I'm going down to lunch.'

'Didn't you have any breakfast?' he asked.

'Not much. In fact, only coffee.'

Lucille turned and left him standing there. Now, somehow, she was angry with him. She wasn't sure why. She only knew one thing: she could no longer be natural with him.

Blair was downstairs before her and already sitting at their table. He rose politely and gave her a long look.

'I've been making some decisions,' he said after they had ordered.

She gave him a startled glance. 'What—what kind of decisions?'

'I'm going to cut this hotel survey short.'

'You mean—just this one?'

'No, the whole project.'

Her throat went dry and she was aware of a great hollow inside which was nothing to do with lack of food.

'But—but why? Is—is it my fault? Is it something I've done—or haven't done? If so——'

Blair shook his head vigorously. 'I'm not prepared to go into reasons with you. Your job will be waiting for you back at my London hotel, so there'll be no problem. Right?'

'I—I—yes, I suppose so,' she stammered. 'When do we return to London?'

'Are you eager to get back? You were when we were in Paris, yet you don't look particularly pleased at the idea now. Or are you hiding your true feelings?'

'I'm not sure what I feel. In any case, I have no say in the matter, have I?'

He did not answer for a moment, then he said quietly, 'I'll tell you what my plan is, then you can please yourself whether you agree or not. But I don't think we should prolong this project. There's one—or rather two—particular hotels I'd like to see. One is in Florence, and as you know the language your help would be invaluable. The other I'd like to see is in Switzerland, and of course the language there could be either French, German,

Italian, or what have you. So, taking travel and stays into consideration, that should take a couple of weeks or so.'

He waited for her reply. Lucille was a mixture of feelings, and didn't quite know what to say. She did not want to curtail their time together. Once this project was finished she might never see Blair again. And yet being in such close proximity as they had been ever since they had left London, and especially since their stay in Paris, was becoming more than she could bear. She had been a fool, she knew, to allow her feelings to get out of hand, but she had never met anyone like him before, had never loved anyone like this before.

'Well?' he prompted. 'Are you willing to carry on for a couple of weeks or not?'

Her eyes flashed for a moment. 'It's you who are cutting the project short, not I.'

'I have my reasons.'

'So you said before,' she came back with some heat. 'All right—whatever you say. After all, you're the boss. I'm—sorry it has to be cut short, but——'

'Are you? Well, we'll get down to Florence and see how we go from there. And now let's talk about something else. There's to be a concert in the courtyard of the Doge's Palace this evening. I thought you might like to go, so I bought two tickets. You're not obliged to go, of course,' he added, 'I can always give one ticket away or——'

'Yes, I—I would like to go,' Lucille said swiftly before he could say anything more. She felt she should apologise for last night. Perhaps he hadn't intended to touch her at all. She had been stupid. A schoolgirl wouldn't have behaved in such a naïve fashion. But she knew instinctively that Blair would not want to discuss the incident on the balcony.

'Good,' he said. 'Then I'll leave you to your own devices this afternoon and see you at dinner. The usual time will do.'

She spent a miserable afternoon, hurt that he had not asked her to go with him, still deeply regretting her panic action last night—which had obviously led to his decision to cut short their travels. The only thing she could do now was behave as though nothing had happened. She imagined he would be most unlikely to touch her ever again.

They had dinner, then made their way to the Doge's Palace, and it was plain that Blair was very much on his guard. He made no attempt either to take her hand or guide her in any way as they crossed the bridges. He simply warned her here and there to 'watch out', or 'mind where you're putting your feet'. She wanted so much to reach out to him, and was tempted once even to pretend to stumble in the hope that he would come to her assistance.

Seats had been erected in the courtyard of the Palace, and there was an air of excitement as, the seats all taken, the members of the orchestra began to take their seats.

'Do you like good music?' asked Blair.

'Oh yes. I've got quite a good selection of records in my flat, and go to concerts whenever possible.'

He looked surprised at her enthusiasm, and went on to ask her about her favourite composer and whether or not she liked opera and so on.

It was good to know they had a common interest, but as the conductor raised his baton Lucille could not help feeling how hopeless it was. In a few weeks' time they would go their separate ways. Later, as they walked into the hotel, Blair was called to the reception desk.

'You're wanted on the telephone,' Lucille interpreted. 'A Miss Gregory.'

Immediately his face lit up as he went across to the telephone. Despondently Lucille went upstairs to her room. It would be the woman who had rung him when they were having lunch at the hotel in Paris. The one he had called 'darling'.

In her room Lucille buried her face in her hands. She had no idea that being in love could be like this—a pain one minute, a joy the next. But mostly pain when the love was not returned.

It was already almost midnight. Having had very little sleep the night before, Lucille fell asleep almost as soon as her head touched the pillow.

They set out for Florence shortly after breakfast, going through Padua and Bologna, where they had lunch. As usual, Blair did not talk much while driving, and to keep her mind from dwelling too much on him, Lucille tried to take an interest in the passing scenery and the smaller towns and villages through which they passed.

To her delight their hotel overlooked the River Arno, with a very good view of the Ponte Vecchio. At least there was from Lucille's room. Whether by accident or design her room was on the first floor, but Blair's on the third. He was taking no chances on being near her this time, she thought with a leaden heart.

They had tea in the elegant lounge on the ground floor. Lucille thought it was simply fantastic that Blair was in the financial position to be able to buy these kind of hotels.

'This is not your first visit to Florence, I take it?' Blair remarked.

She shook her head. 'I've been a couple of times, but I shouldn't think anyone ever gets tired of Florence. It has an atmosphere all its own.'

'Would you like to live here?'

Lucille smiled. 'Well—no, I don't think so. I love my own country too much to want to live anywhere else, even in a place as beautiful as Florence. But it's nice to come back on a visit. How long are we staying here?'

He looked at her in silence for a moment or two, and she wished she knew what was going on in his mind.

'Oh, just long enough to find out what the service and everything is like.'

'Is this hotel on the tourist list, do you know?'

'I shouldn't think so. Private bookings mostly, I should say. Of course, most of the guests will be out either on business or sightseeing, but as a general rule it's easy to identify package tour guests.'

'How?' she asked curiously.

'Well, how do you think?' he returned.

Lucille thought for a moment. 'By the way they dress? The women in short-sleeved florals, the men in shirts they probably wouldn't be seen dead in at home.'

'That's right.'

'Why do you think the hotel is on the market if it's a going concern?' she asked.

Blair shrugged. 'There are many reasons why an individual or company wants to sell. Maybe they need the cash. An individual might want to retire from the hotel business. Some hoteliers think there's more security in the block bookings of the tour operators, and I dare say they're right. But Florence attracts a good many people who don't always travel in a crowd. There are art students, businessmen, those who just love foreign travel and, of course, holidaymakers.'

'So you're classing tourists as those who travel through a tour operator, and holidaymakers as something entirely different.'

'Well, yes. Those on package tours, for example, arrive in bunches of anything from fifty to a hundred. You must have been in hotels yourself when there's what seems like an invasion. With crowds of people all arriving at the same time, all pushing to get at the reception desk to get their keys, luggage and people everywhere so that you can't move, guests fractious and tired after a long journey. You've either got to have a completely tourist—or package tour—hotel or the other kind, the mixture I've already mentioned. And this hotel, if the service and facilities are up to standard, or can easily be improved without too much effort and additional expense, would better suit private individuals.'

Lucille suddenly became aware that he had stopped speaking and was obviously waiting for some comment from her. She had only been half listening. She had been watching his face as he spoke, the different expressions which flitted across his features, the look in his eyes, and most of all the movement of his lips. With a shake of her head she brought herself out of her trancelike state.

Blair misinterpreted her movement. 'You don't agree?'

'Oh—oh yes,' she answered swiftly. 'At least, I agree that you can't mix the two kinds of guests successfully. From what I've seen of it so far, this is a lovely hotel— the furniture and furnishings in the traditional Florentine style one would expect, in what is practically the art centre of the world. Package tours are cheaper than travelling privately, of course, which is why so many people take advantage of them. Some people just couldn't afford to travel otherwise. So, in a way, I think it's a pity that they miss a hotel like this and have to stay in great modern hotels which are all very much like one another.'

Blair gave her what she read as a cynical look. 'Your concern for the less well-off does you credit,' he said. 'But I have a business to run.'

'Of course,' she answered with a certain amount of sarcasm. Hitting back at him from time to time was the only outlet she had for the love she was nurturing for him.

He gave her a look which seemed to say, 'What's the good of arguing with you?' And indeed, they had already discussed the business of money-making. He thought she cared nothing for money and considered him mercenary. At the same time he thought, cynically, that she was hypocritical about money, that in reality she liked the things money could buy.

'Would you like to drive around for a little while before dinner?' he asked. 'Perhaps a run up to the Piazzale Michelangelo?'

Her eyes sparkled with interest. 'Oh yes, I would. It's my favourite spot in Florence.'

Lucille felt that the Piazzale Michelangelo was one of the most beautiful places in the world. It was not so much the square itself, but the magnificent view it gave of the city spread out below. From here could be seen the magnificent cupola of the great cathedral, the bell tower and the Baptistry; the lovely terracotta of the rooftops; the winding river Arno, while rising in the background the seven hills of Florence, and a flurry of greenery in the foreground. With Blair by her side, Lucille felt she could stand here for ever. Wherever she went and whatever she did, she would remember these moments for the rest of her life.

After a while they strolled around the square, and in the centre stopped to look at the bronze copy of Michelangelo's statue of David with the accompanying symbolic statues of Day, Night, Dawn and Dusk.

'Isn't it the most beautiful piece of sculpture you ever saw?' breathed Lucille.

Blair nodded. 'I suppose you've seen the original in the Accademia?'

'Yes, and I'd like to look at it again while we're here.'

'Well, I think that can be arranged,' he said with a hint of a smile. 'But tell me, what strikes you most about it?'

'The head, I think—especially the view from the front we're looking at now—that half-profile. It wouldn't have been nearly so effective if Michelangelo had put the head straight. As it is, David has his head turned slightly and is gazing into the distance.'

'You know there was some criticism of it when it was first put in the Piazza della Signoria? Some said it was too big—it's over thirteen feet high, and David was only supposed to be thirteen years of age. And others thought the right hand too big and criticised the way the veins stood out.'

Lucille laughed. 'But that's ridiculous. A statue doesn't have to be actually life-size—it wouldn't have been nearly so impressive. But I suppose present-day Italians think differently. As to the right hand—surely it's a well-known fact that if your hand is held down the veins *do* fill, just as Michelangelo has fashioned it. The veins don't stand out in the other hand because it's held up. The sculptor, of course, knew his anatomy, whereas his critics of the day didn't.'

'Hm. Well, you seem knowledgeable enough. You do know there are other statues of David?'

'Yes. Donatello did one in bronze, though I haven't seen the original. It's in the Bargello Museum, I believe. But then there's so much to see in Florence. His David is more relaxed, pensive, head down, and wearing a hat. And then I think there's the Young David, also in bronze, by Verrocchio. Both are excellent, of course, and do depict a young boy. One is dressed, the other a nude like this. But somehow or other the Michelangelo has something the others haven't. Again, I think it's the head, the proud tilt, the determination. If there was ever a work of perfection this is it.'

'Mm—very good. You're quite the expert on sculpture, aren't you?'

This Lucille denied modestly. But the David had always held a fascination for her.

She sensed an easing of the tension between Blair and herself, and was glad of it. Just as long as he did not touch her, she could maintain some degree of equilibrium, she hoped.

Back at the hotel, there was just time to unpack and dress for dinner. Blair had arranged to meet her downstairs in the hotel bar, instead of calling for her as he had done sometimes previously. Perhaps it was just as well, she told herself.

She wore a simple black dress for the evening, not long, but sleeveless, topped by the evening jacket she had worn in Paris. She sighed and gave an involuntary shiver as the memory of that evening came flooding back. She would never forget standing there before him, her dress around her ankles, not moving a muscle.

Trying to thrust the image to the back of her mind, she went downstairs. She was taken aback on entering the lounge-bar to see Blair sitting with a very beautiful woman. Lucille's heart plummeted as she saw his relaxed, happy face. She halted in her tracks, not being quite sure whether she would be intruding by joining them. Then Blair saw her and beckoned her to come. As she walked across the room Lucille's gaze was riveted to the other woman. She was dressed most strikingly entirely in white in a sort of Grecian style—a crossover bodice, the skirt flowing elegantly to her ankles, a golden belt at the waist, her blonde hair swept back off her face. Her make-up was perfect.

Blair rose as Lucille approached them from his seat side by side with his companion on an elegant settee.

'Ah, there you are, Lucille. Sit down and I'll get you a drink. By a simply amazing coincidence, I've met an old friend. Caroline, this is Lucille who's travelling with me as my—assistant. Lucille, Lady Caroline St Vincent.'

'Oh,' said Lucille, taken by surprise. But she recovered swiftly. She had spoken to plenty of titled people in the course of her job. 'Good evening, Lady Caroline.' She made no attempt to shake hands; some instinct told her not to. As it was, the other woman made no effort either, and merely inclined her head in acknowledgement.

'Oh, drop the "Lady" and sit down,' Blair said to Lucille, and beckoned a hovering waiter.

'So you're Blair's secretary, are you?' Lady Caroline said smoothly.

'His assistant,' corrected Lucille.

'Oh yes, his assistant. I gather you worked in his London hotel. I'd hate that, being behind a counter and dealing with difficult hotel guests.'

Lucille felt her anger rising. It was obvious that this woman was trying to put her in her place—wherever that might be.

'Actually,' she answered, 'I'm a linguist. That's why Blair asked me to come with him on this trip.'

'Oh, really?' the other came back in a tone which sounded uninterested and at the same time disbelieving. Then she turned deliberately to Blair. 'Darling, I think it's absolutely wonderful that you're thinking of buying my favourite hotel in Florence. And I'm so glad, too, that you're not going to allow the tourists to come in and take over. I haven't anything against people who have to travel on package tours, but they do tend to lower the tone of a place.'

Lucille thought her the most objectionable and condescending person she'd ever met, and hoped Blair wouldn't agree with her. The waiter brought Lucille's drink at that moment, however, so his attention was diverted by paying the man. At any rate, he made no direct reply to some of Lady Caroline's more odious remarks.

'Well, I hope it will remain your favourite hotel,' he said. 'We have yet to sample the food and test the service and accommodation.'

'But, darling, I can assure you it's all first rate—otherwise I shouldn't stay here, you can depend on it.'

But Blair was looking across the room and trying to attract the attention of a man who had just come in. He was a tall, good-looking man of about thirty. Seeing him, Lady Caroline waved too, and Lucille found herself hoping he would turn out to be her husband. She was to be disappointed, however. When he joined them he was introduced to Lucille as David Stevens.

'The Hon.,' added Caroline.

David laughed as he shook hands with Lucille. 'Oh, very honourable—I don't think!' He sat down next to Lucille. 'I say, Blair, what a lucky fellow you are having such a good-looking assistant.'

Lucille smiled. 'Thank you. Are you in Florence on holiday, Mr Stevens?'

He grimaced. 'Oh, not "Mr"—please. Well, not really a holiday. Caroline and I just flew over for the weekend.'

Lucille couldn't help wondering what exactly their relationship was. Perhaps Blair would tell her later—if an opportunity arose. At the moment, Caroline was saying, 'Of course, we *must* have dinner together.'

David agreed with enthusiasm, and Blair nodded agreement too, so Lucille had no option but to nod and smile her own assent.

During dinner David paid her a great deal of attention, and as Caroline monopolised Blair for a greater part of the time, Lucille was almost glad of it. But her heart was heavy as she saw how successful the other girl was in making him smile. Lady Caroline was, of course, a much more suitable person for him than Lucille herself.

They were leaving the restaurant when David caught Lucille's arm as they followed behind the other two.

'Let's go for a walk, shall we? Those two obviously want to be together. Let's leave them to it.'

'But don't you mind that Caroline and Blair are so—so friendly?'

He laughed. 'Good lord, no! In any case, we can show them we can play that game too. I'm not all that keen on foursomes myself. Pairing off is almost inevitable.'

But Lucille didn't want to be 'paired off' with anyone except Blair.

'Come on,' coaxed David, seeing her hesitation. 'Let's make them jealous, if nothing else. I think you—er—rather care for Blair, don't you?'

She denied it a little too swiftly. David gave an understanding smile and put his arm across her shoulders. At that moment Blair looked back, presumably to see if they were coming, but he turned quickly back to Caroline. If only it were remotely possible to make him jealous, Lucille thought miserably. But you were only jealous of someone you really loved. And she was nothing to Blair.

By the time Lucille and David left the restaurant, Caroline and Blair were already seated at a coffee table, deep in conversation.

'Wait here,' suggested David. 'I'll go and tell them we're going. There's no point in both of us walking over. I doubt if they'll stop talking long enough to listen, anyway.'

He did not realise how every word was like a knife through her heart. She would be glad to get outside, and away from them. She watched as David spoke to them. Blair stopped listening to Caroline long enough to nod and give the briefest of glances her way.

'Have they known each other long?' she asked David when he rejoined her.

'For some time, I think, but Blair takes a lot of pinning down. He's had a number of women, but none have succeeded in capturing him so far. He *is* quite a good catch, you know.'

'Money-wise, you mean?'

'Well, yes. And he's a thoroughly nice bloke into the bargain.'

'You've known him a long time?' Lucille asked.

'We were at school together.'

'Tell me—what was he like then?' asked Lucille as they stepped outside. She wanted to know as much about him as possible.

David put his hand under her arm. 'Oh, he was a good all-rounder. You name it, he was good at it. And no one ever got the better of him.'

Lucille laughed shortly. 'I can well imagine that!'

He gave her a sidelong glance. 'Had one or two ups and downs with him, have you?'

'Sort of. But he always wins.'

'Ah yes, but one of these days Blair will meet a woman who'll be more than a match for him.'

'He seems to have someone special now,' she told him. 'He rings her—or she him—at every hotel where we stay.'

'Really? I wouldn't know. Actually, I haven't seen him for years until I ran into him here up on the third floor before dinner. But let's talk about you. Surely you've got some man lined up somewhere?'

'Not really.'

'I don't believe it.' They had reached the Ponte Vecchio, and David stopped and pulled her round to face him. 'You're a very attractive woman, do you know that?'

Lucille thought fleetingly that she would give anything to hear Blair say something like that to her. She shook her head modestly.

'You are, you know,' he insisted, and bent his head and kissed her. It was a light, friendly kiss, and Lucille did nothing to prevent his arms going about her. Somehow she found a degree of comfort in the arms of this amiable man. She leaned her head on his shoulder seeking solace, and he held her for a moment. Then his lips sought hers again, this time with more ardour. But this was something she didn't want from anyone except Blair.

She pushed against him. 'No—please. Let's walk on, shall we?'

He laughed and let her go. 'What are you afraid of?'

'I'm not afraid of anything.'

'You are. You're not happy, are you? Is it Blair? It wouldn't surprise me in the least.'

'What makes you say that?' she stalled defensively.

'Oh, I caught you looking at him once or twice—and at Caroline. You were jealous, my pet—and rather down in the mouth.'

Lucille sighed. 'I shall be glad when this trip's over. It was to have gone on for six months, but Blair has cut it short.'

'Why has he?' asked David.

'He wouldn't give any reason. We—have had one or two differences of opinion. Perhaps that's the reason.'

David laughed outright. 'You don't mean to tell me you actually stood up to him? I know how stubborn he can be.'

Lucille made no reply. They made their way slowly across the bridge, pausing now and then to look at some of the jewellery displayed in the shop windows on either side. These had the same interest for Lucille as they had for many women.

'But all too expensive for me, I'm afraid,' she sighed.

'My dear girl,' David answered in a pained voice, 'women don't buy their own jewellery! It's not expected of them.'

Lucille laughed. 'Well, I can't think of anyone who'd buy such fabulous stuff for me.'

'Can't you?' he murmured. 'Pity the shops aren't open, I'd buy you something myself.'

'You!' she exclaimed incredulously. 'But I could never accept such a gift.'

'Why ever not? I've got pots of money. Not quite as much as Blair, perhaps, but enough. I wouldn't miss a thousand or so for a necklace or bracelet. You mustn't be so old-fashioned, Lucille. Men don't necessarily expect what the Victorians used to call "favours", if they bought a woman a present.'

'Don't they?' Lucille asked sceptically.

'Anyway——' David stopped and pulled her round to face him again, oblivious of strolling couples all around them, 'I'd like to marry you. What do you say?'

Lucille gave a startled gasp. 'Oh, don't be silly!'

'I'm not being silly. I'm serious.'

'You can't be. You haven't known me for five minutes.'

'It's enough—and it's two or three hours,' he corrected. 'It's long enough to know what kind of woman you are.'

Lucille disengaged herself from his embrace and began to walk back the way they had come. But he was not to be put off so easily. He stopped her again.

'Don't you like me?' he asked.

'Of course I do. But liking isn't enough for marriage.'

'You'd come to it. I'd make you.'

She laughed and shook her head. 'Let's change the subject. It's silly to go on talking this way. I'd rather not.'

'There's such a thing as love at first sight, you know.'

She stared at him. 'You're not trying to tell me that you——'

'Why not? As soon as I saw you, I thought: there's the woman for me.'

But Lucille couldn't accept that. 'A first-sight attraction isn't necessarily love. No, please, David. It's impossible.'

'You said you liked me, and that's a start,' he persisted. 'Is it that there's someone else—back in London, perhaps?'

'Well, no—not really.'

'Then it must be Blair,' he decided.

Lucille gave an exasperated sigh. 'David, just because I don't want to marry you—even supposing you really were being serious—why should you assume that it's because I've already got someone else?'

He grimaced. 'It usually follows. But I suppose I've been too quick for you. Promise me you'll think about it.'

But she shook her head. 'David, you've spoken on some impulse. You'd regret it in the morning if I said yes. And I must be honest with you. There *is* someone else. It's hopeless, but I couldn't possibly marry anyone else feeling as I do. It wouldn't be fair. I—I dare say I'll get over it in time,' she finished. But at the present moment she felt convinced that she never would 'get over' loving Blair. 'Anyway,' she added in a different tone, trying to banish unhappy thoughts, 'what about you and Lady Caroline? Why don't you marry her?'

'For the simple reason that she's married already,' he said lightly.

'And you've come away with her for the weekend? Does her husband know?'

He laughed. 'There you go again, little Miss Victorian! In this day and age, and certainly in our set, husbands and wives don't live in each other's pockets, even if they live in one house.'

'Oh really? Well, that's not my idea of marriage. I'd want to marry purely for love, and people who love each other don't want to do things separately. I wouldn't want my husband to fool around with other women, and I would certainly be faithful. You can call me Victorian or anything else you like.'

David gave a long and indulgent laugh. 'Darling, you're a wonder! Love in a cottage is your ideal, is it?'

Love anywhere with Blair, she thought. They were nearing the hotel, having only been out for about an hour. David protested that it was too early to go in yet, but Lucille pleaded that she was tired. A swift glance around the various lounges and bars showed no sign of Blair.

'Perhaps they've gone out,' suggested David. 'Or maybe they're up in Caroline's suite.'

Lucille gave him a startled glance. 'But Blair wouldn't——' she protested hotly, then halted in confusion. Blair had had no compunction about sharing a suite with herself.

David laughed softly. 'You are a silly! Blair has quite a reputation with women. If it's him you're in love with, I'd forget him, if I were you.'

Lucille compressed her lips as she walked towards the lift. The ache in her heart was almost unbearable. All she wanted to do now was get to the privacy of her own room.

She had reached her door when she realised that David was still with her. She turned to him to say goodnight as she put her key in the lock.

'Let me come in and kiss you goodnight properly,' he said softly. 'We can't do it out here in the corridor.'

He already had his arm about her shoulders. Lucille wanted to cry. She was in no mood to do battle against either him or anyone. If only he would just go and leave her in peace!

The door clicked open and she turned to David to say a firm goodnight. But over his shoulder she saw Blair appear, only to halt at the sight of her. Before she could shake herself free of David's arm he had turned and walked away again.

'Please, David, let me go!' she said raggedly. 'I'm tired and I just want to be alone.'

She went swiftly into her room and closed the door almost in his face. She heard him call out goodnight, then presumed he had gone. Becoming more and more worn out by the minute, she almost went to sleep in the bath. As a result, she fell asleep as soon as her head touched the pillow.

It was still dark when she next opened her eyes after tossing about for a while feeling too warm. There seemed to be a peculiar glow showing between the curtains at the window. They would be the lights of the city, she

thought. But it certainly was warm. She closed her eyes
and tried to go to sleep again, throwing back the top
blanket. But then she could hear a strange noise. She
sat up in bed and pressed the switch of her bedside lamp,
but nothing happened—and then she became aware of
a curious orange light showing underneath her door.

She sniffed. There was a smell of burning. And what
was that crackling noise? She drew in a swift breath of
fear. Something was on fire. The hotel—the hotel was
on fire! She must warn someone. She picked up her
bedside telephone, but could get no response.

Really afraid now, she slipped on her dressing-gown
and went to open her door. But a searing flame met her
and she swiftly closed it. She glanced around the room
and ran her fingers along the walls of the small corridor
leading from the bedroom to her bathroom. Surely there
was a fire-extinguisher somewhere? But her searching
fingers found nothing.

The smoke coming under the door began to make her
cough. The heat from the door was unbearable. She
backed away from it and stared for a moment as the
flame slowly ate its way through the heavy wood, and
the next moment she gave a horrified yell as a panel gave
way and the flames shot into the room. For a moment
Lucille felt panic-stricken. She backed further into the
room, but the smoke and fumes followed her.

She glanced at the window—her only means of escape.
Then, trying to keep her head, she pulled on a pair of
slacks over her nightdress, tucking it in, and pulled on
a sweater.

A wet towel, that was the thing, she thought wildly.
But when she tried to get to the bathroom, the flames
and smoke drove her back. She next tried to open the
window a little further, but it was jammed. Although
there was a small balcony outside, it was obviously more
ornamental than anything else, and she could only con-
clude that the window was jammed with paint.

She looked around for something to break the glass with. The heel of one of her shoes—that was the thing. By now she was choking and her eyes swimming with tears as smoke filled them. Her chest painful, she hammered at the window. It was more difficult to break than she would have imagined. Somewhere at the back of her mind was the feeling that you were not supposed to open windows when there was a fire. Air either sucked the fire out or blew it in. But she had to get out somehow, and the window was the only way.

She became aware of noise now—lots of noise. People shouting, sirens screaming. At last she managed to break the window, but by now she was gasping for breath, her senses swimming. Then she sank to the ground and her senses left her.

CHAPTER NINE

LUCILLE became vaguely aware of hands touching her, of someone talking to her. Still in a state of semi-consciousness, she imagined she was calling Blair's name, yet she was aware that only the merest croak was coming out of her parched throat. She clung desperately to whoever it was who was in the room with her.

'Thank God I've found you in time!' a voice said. There was a breaking of glass and she felt a breath of cool, fresh air on her face. Then she felt herself being lifted up bodily.

'If you can hear me, keep perfectly still,' the voice commanded her. It sounded like Blair, but it couldn't be, she thought. It must be a fireman.

Out on the balcony, she was lifted over the man's shoulder and carried slowly and carefully down a ladder. All around was noise and confusion and the sound of water being hosed on the fire. On the ground she was wrapped in blankets and placed face downwards as someone began artificial respiration on her. Then she was lifted on to a stretcher, and opened her eyes to see Blair sitting beside her in an ambulance.

Realising how near she had come to losing her life, she held out her arms to him. 'Oh, Blair——'

Tears flooded out of her aching eyes as the tension within her broke. Swiftly Blair put his arms about her.

'It's all right, darling, you're safe now,' he said soothingly. 'Thank God you had the sense to put on some warm clothing and get near the window. Another few minutes and the floor would have given way.'

'But—but how did you—get—get in?' she gasped, recalling the flames which had blocked the door to her room. Surely he hadn't—— She tried to look at his face, but the light in the ambulance was rather dim, and the vision of her tear-filled and smarting eyes was not very good.

Blair laid her head back on the small pillow. 'Just close your eyes and lie still. Don't try to talk. You're going to the local hospital for treatment. You need rest and oxygen.'

Still frightened and in need of comfort, Lucille put out her hand to him.

'Blair, don't leave me—please!'

He took her hand and held it firmly in his. 'I won't. Now, don't worry. Everything's going to be all right.'

She closed her eyes, and felt her senses leave her again at his reassurance. But before long she seemed to be back in the hot, smoke-filled hotel bedroom, trying to get out and screaming Blair's name. She awoke to feel his soothing hand on her forehead.

'We're there now—at the hospital. They'll give you a sedative, then you'll sleep, and when you waken it will all be over.'

Five minutes later she was in a warm bed, had been given an injection and had an oxygen mask over her mouth and nose.

'Now go to sleep,' Blair told her. 'And I'll be here when you wake up, make no mistake about that.'

Lucille was just able to notice his burnt and tattered clothing before she fell headlong into a dreamless sleep.

As he had promised, he was still sitting beside her bed when she awoke, but this time he was wearing a dressing gown. Her oxygen mask had been taken away.

'I slept for a while in the next room,' he told her.

She frowned, remembering the state of his trousers. 'Were you burned? You must have been. How on earth did you get through that fire into my room?'

'I draped my face in a wet towel, topped that with my jacket and just charged in. It was the only way. I must say the fire precautions in that hotel are simply abysmal! No fire-doors——'

'And no fire-extinguishers—I tried to find one. But, Blair, you couldn't cover yourself all over. You must have been terribly burnt.'

He shook his head. 'Not too badly. I've had some treatment. I'm a very peculiar colour in places, I can tell you!'

She was sure he was making light of it all. She looked at him, tears of gratitude welling up in her eyes, and her love for him more than she could bear.

'Blair——' she choked, 'you saved my life.'

'Well, someone had to, didn't they?' he said casually. 'Besides, you being my—assistant, I had what you might call a vested interest in you. I'm sure anyone would have done the same. The Honourable David, for instance.'

'David!' Lucille coloured as she remembered how Blair had seen them outside her door. 'He didn't come into my room,' she told him vehemently.

'I know. All the same, he's pretty smitten with you. He tells me he wants to marry you.'

'Well, I don't want to marry him.'

Blair shrugged. 'You could do worse.'

'And I could do better,' she flashed back. 'I don't want a man who runs around with other men's wives!'

'My dear girl, it's done all the time in their set. Nobody thinks anything of it.'

'Don't they? Well, I do.'

Lucille was hurt and disturbed that he should be talking like this. If only he showed the slightest regard for her! He had been kind, he had saved her life, but obviously he wouldn't worry in the slightest if she married someone else. And why should he? Because she loved him, that didn't mean he must love her. Far from it. He had simply no idea how she felt about him.

'You'd be forever the faithful wife, I suppose?' Blair said with more than a hint of sarcasm.

'Yes, I would!' she hurled back. 'And if that's what you call puritan or Victorian or whatever, then yes, that's what I am, and that's what I'd be. I suppose you're in that set too?' she finished, feeling thoroughly wound up and frustrated.

He raised his eyebrows. 'You've certainly recovered, haven't you?' He rose. 'I should think I can safely leave you now. I'm waiting for someone to bring me some clothes, then we can be on our way.'

'What do you mean—on our way? Are we going back to the hotel? How much damage was done? You haven't told me anything yet!'

Blair sat down again. 'The fire started in the kitchens. Your room is directly above, along with a few others. I don't know whether we can salvage any of your clothes— probably not. I suggest we go to another hotel for one night—you won't be fit to travel today. Tomorrow, all being well, we go to Switzerland. There's a hotel there I really must see and which I'd like to buy.'

'What about the one here in Florence? Was there much damage?'

'A fair amount. It's something I'll have to think about. I either buy it cheaply and do the renovating myself or see it when all the damage has been repaired, *and* proper fire precautions installed, such as fire-doors and alarms. But that will undoubtedly put the price up. The hotel's insurance might cover it, of course—if they've got such a thing.'

The door opened at this juncture, and David stood there, a winning smile on his face.

'Can I come in? The nurse said it was all right.'

Blair rose to his feet immediately. 'Come in, by all means. That is, if the lady wishes to see you—and I'm sure she does.'

Lucille smiled her assent. She was really pleased to see him.

At the door Blair turned. 'I'll be back just as soon as my clothes arrive and I've found out about yours, Lucille.'

'Were the ones I was wearing badly burned or damaged?'

'Not burned, but drenched and not exactly as you'd like,' he answered, and disappeared.

David thrust some gorgeous flowers into her hands and bent to kiss her.

'How are you? You poor little thing, what a terrible experience for you! Blair saved your life, do you know?'

She nodded. 'He makes light of it, of course. It's a mercy he wasn't burned more. But his face is hardly touched. I don't understand it.'

'He had the sense to cover his face. The lower part of his body will be worst, and his legs and feet. We tried to tackle the fire in the corridor, but he wouldn't wait. He put his head down and made a mad dash. It's all here in the morning papers—look.'

David pulled out a paper from under his arm, and there it was in large headlines on the front page: *Gallant Englishman saves girl's life.* Lucille read it all, translating automatically as she went along.

Tears filled her eyes. 'How perfectly awful! I shall never be able to thank him enough. May I keep this?'

David nodded. 'I bought it especially for you.' He inclined his head and examined her face. 'What a miracle that that lovely face of yours isn't marked. That would have been terrible.'

'I was over by the window,' she explained. 'It hadn't reached there. The fire must have started in the corridor, and I couldn't get out through the door. I tried to break the window, but the smoke got into my lungs and I—must have passed out.'

David was looking at her oddly. 'Lucille, why don't you give Blair some hint as to the way you feel about him?'

She stared at him. 'Oh, no, I couldn't!'

'Why not? Men sometimes need a little encouragement.'

But she shook her head firmly. 'For one thing, there *is* another woman, I'm convinced of it. And if I made any kind of overtures to him and he turned me down I'd just die. It's bad enough as it is.'

'I don't think he would turn you down.'

A deep sense of misery consumed her as she recalled that night in Paris. 'He already has, but I don't want to talk about it,' she answered.

'But what happened?' David persisted with a puzzled frown.

'Well—he made certain advances and I didn't resist. Then he suddenly turned away. Now please, David, no more——' Her lips quivered. She put her hand to her mouth and with a great effort prevented herself from bursting into tears.

David's hand shot out. 'I'm sorry, darling. Don't upset yourself. The man's an idiot, and he doesn't deserve you. I've half a mind to tell him so.'

Her eyes widened with alarm. 'Oh, don't! If you as much as give him a hint, I'll never forgive you. I'd deny it if he asked me, anyway, so nothing would be gained. You'd only make matters worse.'

'All right, all right,' he said soothingly, 'don't get yourself into a tizz. I know one thing—I simply wouldn't be able to resist you.'

Lucille made no reply. Every word David said was like a knife through her heart. Blair could certainly resist her—and had done so when other men could simply not have held back, having gone so far, even had they not actually been in love.

Blair returned, and with him he brought a dress belonging to Lady Caroline.

Lucille eyed it with distaste. She knew in her heart that the feeling was sheer prejudice. It was a beautiful and an expensive dress, there was no doubt whatever about that.

'Was there nothing left of my own clothes?' she asked.

Blair shook his head. 'Caroline said to tell you that the dress is absolutely new and hasn't been worn. You're to accept it as a gift. I had no idea of your size or I'd have gone and bought you something,' he went on, seeing her doubtful expression. 'Caroline thought you'd be about her size. She's also included a new pair of tights, and I've bought you some underwear. We can do some shopping before we leave for Switzerland. I can see you're not happy about the dress.'

Lucille began to feel ashamed of her ingratitude. 'I'm sorry—it was very good of Lady Caroline. I must thank her before we go. But I'd like to do some shopping all the same.'

'Of course you would,' agreed Blair. 'Come on, David—out, while the lady gets dressed. We'll see you in the main entrance, Lucille. Just turn right outside your door, along the corridor and then turn left.'

Caroline had been right. The tights were just Lucille's size, and the dress fitted perfectly. So did the expensive underwear. Had Caroline gone with him to buy the things? she wondered. He had not said anything about the sandals he had brought, but they fitted her. She decided to leave the nightdress she had been wearing behind. Of her slacks and sweater she could not see anything.

When she reached the main entrance of the hospital, only Blair was there.

'David has a lunch date with Caroline,' he told her. 'I thought we'd find a restaurant in the shopping area. How are you feeling?'

'I'm fine. But what about you?' she asked anxiously. 'You must have got horribly burned.'

'Not so horribly—I rushed through. It stings a bit, that's all, and I had some treatment while you were asleep, so don't fuss. I've seen the doctor, and he says it's all right for you to leave.'

He took her arm and led her outside to where his car was waiting.

'We'll have lunch first,' he said as he took the wheel. 'Then shopping, after which we'll make a start on the journey. Are you sure you feel fit to travel?'

Lucille assured him she was. It had been a great ordeal, but she felt safe with Blair. 'How far do you expect to get today?' she asked.

'That depends on how long the shopping takes and how you feel. I thought we'd make for the coast road. Perhaps you'd like to stop off at Pisa for a brief look at the Cathedral and Leaning Tower, though I expect you've seen them.'

She told him she wouldn't mind a second look, then suddenly realised that she had no handbag.

'My money!' she wailed. 'I haven't any money. Or traveller's cheques. They're all in my handbag, and goodness knows what's happened to that.'

Blair put his hand on her arm. 'Calm down, Lucille. The traveller's cheques will be no use to anybody. As to the money, I don't suppose you had a fortune, exactly, and so that doesn't matter, either. And we can easily buy you a new handbag. Where was your passport, by the way?'

She relaxed. 'In the hotel reception.'

'That's all right, then. So there are no problems. Your recuperation is all that matters, and you can do that in the hotel in Switzerland. It's a nice hotel. I've stayed there before—that's why I want to buy it.'

She gave him a sidelong glance. 'But if you've already stayed there, why do you want to see it again?'

'I—thought it would be a fitting end to our tour. I had intended leaving it until last, anyway.'

'Do they have vacancies?' Lucille asked.

He nodded. 'A suite and a single. The suite has a view which is out of this world.'

He found a car park, and before they got out of the car he threw a wad of lire notes on to her lap. 'There you are. I suppose you'd prefer to pay for things yourself. Now don't argue, there's a good girl,' he added as she began to protest. 'I owe you far more than that, so come along. I suggest we buy a suitcase first, then we can put the shopping into it.'

Lucille had seldom, if ever, bought a whole wardrobe at the same time. She bought several sets of underwear, nightdresses, négligés, tights, shoes and sandals, cotton dresses, a linen suit, two dinner dresses, a raincoat, jeans and sweaters, and at Blair's insistence, a light but warm coat. She also had to buy new cosmetics and various kinds of toiletries.

'Now, are you sure that's all you're going to need between here and London?' Blair asked, as he put the last of the heaviest items into the suitcase.

'I can't think of anything else,' she told him.

'Right. I'll go and put these things in the car and then we'll have lunch.'

There was something different in Blair's behaviour towards her, and she could only think that he was being extra kind because of her experience in the fire. When they had eaten, they returned to the hotel to settle up and collect their passports. Lucille was shocked at the sight of the hotel. Almost the whole of one corner of the building was black and scarred, including, of course, the room she had occupied. Water and charred wood still lay around and broken glass was everywhere. She stayed in the car while Blair went inside to get their passports and the rest of his luggage. The part of the hotel where he had been staying had remained unaffected.

'I wouldn't feel inclined to buy that, even when it's been repaired,' she offered as he joined her.

'No?' he answered as he flung his luggage on to the back seat. 'Not even if I can buy it cheaply and repair it myself—and put in fire-doors, etc?'

She shook her head. 'Reports of the fire were in the newspapers this morning. The hotel will have a bad name in the kind of circles from where you would draw your customers. It will be a long time before people have sufficient confidence to stay there.'

'So what would you suggest?' Blair asked as he drove off.

'Look out for another one in Florence.'

'A good idea, but not just now. We're on our way to Switzerland, then we shall be returning to London.'

Returning to London. Cutting short the six-month trip. The idea gave Lucille very little joy. Life for her would never be the same again without Blair, for when they returned to London she would probably only see him on the rare occasions when he visited the hotel.

After about an hour and a half they arrived at Pisa, and it was a very pleasant experience to see once again the beautiful Cathedral with its Leaning Tower and Baptistry, all in white marble. It was a most impressive group of buildings, and from one standpoint the Tower, with its sixteen-foot incline from the original vertical, could be seen almost in isolation.

'Various architects keep coming up with ideas of straightening, but I doubt if they ever will,' said Blair.

Lucille laughed. 'It wouldn't be the same if it were straight, would it? And by monkeying about with it, it might topple, and that would be dreadful.'

'Let's hope it doesn't topple, in any case, although it must have driven the architect mad when it began to lean—due, I believe, to a subsidence of the soil.'

With a last lingering look they were on their way again, and Lucille knew that whenever she visited Pisa again it would be with the memory of Blair at her side.

From Pisa they took the coast road and stayed the night at Genoa. It was a place Lucille had never before visited, and after they had had dinner she suggested a walk.

'Sure you feel up to it?' Blair enquired.

She assured him she did, but all the same he took the car to save too much walking, especially up the hills. It was an interesting city with narrow streets and alleys, some of them consisting of flights of stairs and overhung by very tall tenements. The wider streets climbed gradually upwards towards the amphitheatre of hills beyond. They looked at the cathedral of San Lorenzo, the Gothic palace of San Giorgio, and walked under the massive Porto Soprana, part of the medieval city wall. Finally they strolled along the harbour.

It was a warm night, and it was wonderful to be with Blair like this. Lucille was sorely tempted to take his arm, and wished he might put his hand on her shoulder or take her hand. But he did neither, and after a little while he suggested that an early night would be a good idea.

'And let's hope nobody leaves a chip pan on the stove,' he said meaningly.

Lucille echoed the hope. A great tiredness was beginning to take possession of her and she longed for a good night's sleep.

Blair left her at the bottom of the lift. 'I'll be up myself soon,' he told her. 'I just have a telephone call to make. Two, as a matter of fact. I must let people know where we are and where we're going. Sleep well. Don't forget that I'm next door. If you need anything or have bad dreams, give me a knock.'

All she could muster was the ghost of a smile as he pushed her into the lift. She could guess at both telephone calls he was going to make—one to the London hotel, but the other to the woman in his life. She was too tired and dispirited even to weep as she made her way to her room. She thought vaguely of Jim. She really ought to make a telephone call too, to let him know what was happening, but she simply had not the energy or the heart. She would be back in London soon, anyway—perhaps within a week. After a quick wash she slipped between the sheets, and was asleep almost immediately.

She was awakened at eight-thirty by a maid bringing in tea—obviously ordered for her by Blair last night. She sipped it gratefully, and was pouring a second cup when a knock came at the door. Thinking it would be the maid again, she called out 'Come in', but it was Blair who entered. Her heart gave a sudden bound so that she almost spilt the tea. She tried to ignore the fact that one strap of her nightdress had slipped down on to her arm. She did not want to make the mistake again of any defensive gestures.

'How are you feeling?' he asked. 'Did you sleep well?'

'Oh—oh, yes. I slept fine, thank you, and thanks for ordering the tea for me.'

To hide her feelings, she sipped at her tea, but this made her even more aware of the strap of her nightdress, now tight on her upper arm. If she moved in the wrong direction it might even slip down further. A silly thing to be worrying about, she knew, but Blair made her think and do silly things.

'Well, I'll leave you to drink your tea,' he said. 'You—certainly look better this morning. Can you make it down to breakfast in half an hour?'

She said she could, and he went out. Lucille sighed and pulled up her strap. Was she ever going to be able to behave naturally towards him? She told herself it would be a good thing when this project was over, but she knew in her heart that when they went their separate ways she would be desolate.

They started on their journey again shortly after breakfast, leaving the coast road and heading for Turin. They were making, it seemed, for Montreux, and from there would climb upwards to a mountain village some twenty thousand feet above sea level.

'It's the kind of place people go to stay who really want—and need—peace and quiet without boredom. Because I maintain that it's impossible to be bored in such beautiful and majestic surroundings. There are walks and other villages to explore, there are mountains to be climbed; the hotel has its own tennis courts and swimming pool, and in the evenings those who wish can play cards, listen to music, or even dance if they like. Or do just nothing but sit and read or talk.'

Lucille took a deep breath. 'It sounds heavenly.'

'I'm glad you think so. I visualise people like MPs and business men and women visiting the place, those who live their lives at continuous top pitch with all the stresses and strains which result.'

They did not stop at Turin, but pressed on. As they proceeded, the way became more and more mountainous with steep gradients and winding roads. At Châtillon they had lunch, then pressed on, as Blair wanted to reach their destination before nightfall.

As usual, he did not talk very much while driving, and Lucille kept quiet too. Along these steep mountainous roads he needed all his concentration. Had he not already shown himself to be a good driver, fully in command of his vehicle, there were times when Lucille's heart would have been in her mouth as he negotiated some of the bends with very little between them and precipitous falls. But although she realised his need for concentration, Lucille had the oddest feeling that he had something else on his mind as well as his driving. Had it something to do with his telephone calls of the previous evening?

After what seemed an interminable number of bends and twists as they climbed steadily upwards, Blair at last announced that they were almost at their journey's end. He pointed to a hotel which seemed to be standing on top of the world.

'Do you really think anyone will ever want to go up there?' asked Lucille.

'We have, haven't we? Wait until you see the place. Don't worry, we shall be turning people away in a very short time. It's full now, except for the one suite and a single—as I told you. Once a hotel has gained a certain reputation, one hardly needs to advertise.'

'But what about the winter? Won't the hotel be empty for six months out of twelve?'

He shook his head. 'Not necessarily. There are those who like winter holidays. There'll be plenty of skiing around here. The funicular railway line runs as far as Caux, and from there we can clear a road. No problem.'

Around yet another bend and up another steep incline, and they were there.

'Oh, my goodness!' Lucille gasped as she looked up at the place.

'You like it?'

'It's—magnificent. Please—don't tell me how much it's going to cost to buy it. I'm sure I'd faint!'

Blair gave a derisive laugh. 'You're always worrying about how much things cost! I'm more interested in how much money I'm going to make. Believe me, it isn't the poor who are going to come up here. I aim to redecorate the place and put up the prices.'

'And lose some customers?'

'Assuredly not. You'll see.'

He spoke as though she was going to be around to see, Lucille thought. A sort of figure of speech, that was all. The front of the hotel was grand and most imposing. It was stone-built, each room having its own balcony; the windows on the ground floor looked as though they ran from floor to ceiling, and the approach to the doubled-glazed doors was by way of white stone steps which ran the whole width of the hotel.

'It's called the Imperial Hotel,' Blair told her.

'Very apt indeed!'

This time he did put his hand under her elbow as they climbed the steps, and Lucille felt herself shiver under his touch.

Even Blair noticed. 'Cold?' he queried. 'It wouldn't be surprising at this height.'

She shook her head, not trusting herself to speak. At the top of the steps was a patio with seats on either side of the doors, and vividly coloured geraniums and begonias in terracotta containers.

The reception area was equally pleasing. There was a beautifully patterned marble floor, exotic plants and flowers were everywhere in great troughs and on pedestals, and there were comfortable chairs for those who needed to sit and wait.

It was obvious that Blair was expected. Within a few minutes a man came forward to greet them, speaking Blair's name. Blair introduced him as the manager, and a boy was summoned to bring in their luggage.

'And perhaps you would like some tea in the suite, *monsieur*?' the manager, Monsieur Delon, suggested.

Both Blair and Lucille said that would be very acceptable. They were escorted to the first floor and ushered into the most beautiful room with a view that was simply magnificent. Far, far below lay Lake Geneva, placid in the evening sun, and tiny villages clustered up the mountainside, half hidden by a lush growth of pine trees.

'Wait until you see it by night,' Blair told her as he stood at her side on the iron balcony.

'It must be lovely,' Lucille answered. But as this was going to be his quarters, she was not anticipating to see the view from this window.

She was wondering where her own room was situated when the door opened to admit the boy bearing the luggage. At once Lucille saw that he had brought all their luggage, her own as well as Blair's, and she began to protest.

'This isn't right! My luggage should be——'

Blair silenced her with a gesture of arrogance such as she had not seen from him for a few days.

He fished a coin from his pocket and gave it to the boy. 'Thank you, that will be all.'

The boy disappeared quickly. Lucille's heart was racing. She simply could not bear a repetition of what had happened in Paris. She would refuse to share the suite with him.

'Blair, I absolutely refuse——'

He silenced her with a rapier look from his dark eyes. 'You absolutely refuse to what?' he demanded.

'I—I refuse to—to share a suite with you!'

'I'm not asking you to,' he rasped. 'The suite is yours. I'm going to find the single.'

He picked up his one suitcase and went angrily from the room, slamming the door behind him. Lucille stared after him, near to tears. What a fool she had been to jump to conclusions like that! She could not bear his anger. It had been a natural mistake for the boy to bring up all the luggage. Or had the manager been under the impression that they were sharing? They could, in any case, have both used it in the daytime. But it had not occurred to her that Blair would give her the suite and choose the single for himself. At least, she supposed that was what had been in his mind. She wanted to run after him, to apologise, to fling herself at his feet.

A knock on the door brought her back to her senses, and she opened it to see a waitress bearing tea for two with cakes and very English-looking scones.

'Will you try to find Mr Saunders for me?' she asked as the girl put down the tray. 'I don't know his room number, I'm afraid, but the manager will know. And will you tell Mr Saunders that—the tea is ready in the suite.'

'*Oui, madame.*'

Lucille hoped that, by now, his anger would have cooled sufficiently well for him to join her. She could then apologise, and at least he would not remain angry with her. Her mistake had, after all, been a very natural one.

While she was waiting for him she went to the bathroom to wash her hands and tidy herself. But five minutes went by, and Blair did not come. Very tentatively she poured out a cup of tea for herself. He would surely be here soon. A few minutes later the telephone rang, and when she spoke into the receiver, it was the manager.

'I'm afraid, *madame*, that Monsieur Saunders has gone out. He has friends at one of the hotels in Caux, so he has gone there.'

Lucille thanked him, her heart leaden. Blair, it seemed, had friends everywhere he went. It would be a woman, of that she had no doubt. What was it that David had said? 'He's had a number of women.' She did not doubt that either, but it only knotted the pain more than ever in her heart.

At seven o'clock, the telephone rang. It was Blair, to tell her that he would not be joining her for dinner.

'If I were you, I'd have it in the suite,' he advised. 'The hotel is full, but it's a youth organisation. I'll see you some time tomorrow. Everything OK?'

'Yes, thank you,' was all Lucille could say.

He rang off almost before she had finished speaking, and a deep well of despair welled up inside her.

She had a meal in the suite as he had suggested, but had no appetite, and as she picked here and there at the food she could not help re-living the meal they had had together in the suite in Paris.

When she had eaten she put on the coat she had bought in Florence and went for a walk. The main road was either steeply up or steeply down. It was hardly the kind of terrain for walking, and she did not really feel like mountain-climbing. Her energy was being sapped by her inner torment. And besides, she thought ironically, she had not the right footwear.

She went down the road a little way, hoping perhaps that she might come across a footpath which might lead across the mountain instead of either up or down, or was curved in such a way as to render steepness less noticeable. She continued down for a little while, keeping well to the side of the road as the occasional car roared up or ran down. Now and then she stopped to look around at the view, awe-inspiring and at the same time a balm to the senses. Then at last she found a footpath. Deciding she had better not go too far and get lost, otherwise Blair might have to send out a search party for her, and it was already almost dark, she left the main road and walked along for a while. Part of the footpath ran alongside a belt of trees, and she was just thinking to herself that she ought to be turning back, when suddenly a man jumped out from the trees. Lucille screamed and started to run, and it was then she realised that it was darker than she had realised. She missed her footing and fell headlong, then as her head hit a hidden rock she passed out.

She awoke to feel someone examining her head and muttering curses. Opening her eyes, she was about to scream again for help, but the face a few inches from hers was Blair's.

He glared at her. 'How often have I told you not to go wandering around strange places alone?' he demanded. 'I can't leave you alone for five minutes! Are you all right?' he added, almost as though it was merely an afterthought.

'Yes, I—I think so. And there's no need to be so angry!' she flung. 'What am I supposed to do? Sit twiddling my fingers? A man jumped out at me. How was I to know that in a place like this, men would be lurking behind every tree waiting to pounce on innocent people?'

'Don't be ridiculous! That was me. And I wasn't lurking, I'd been for a walk. Come on, get up if you can and we'll get back to the hotel. I think the best thing I can do is to see you tucked up in bed where you'll be safe.'

She was about to retort that that was the last thing she would allow him to do, but he was already helping her to her feet, and his touch robbed her of words. He took her arm and guided her back the way she had come, watching her every step. By the time they reached the hotel she was feeling more like flinging her arms around his neck and declaring her love for him.

'It—it was very good of you to let me have the suite, and take the single for yourself,' she told him in a contrite tone of voice.

'You really wouldn't expect me to do anything else, would you?' he answered.

'I'm afraid I did. After all, you're the boss.'

Blair threw back his head and gave an explosive laugh. 'Nobody would think so, to hear you going on sometimes!'

'Well, you're not such an easy boss to get along with,' she retorted.

He grunted. 'You haven't really seen me in action yet.'

Lucille thought to herself that, in that case, she hoped she never would.

'You—you missed your tea, you know,' she reminded him. 'I sent someone to look for you, but you were not to be found.'

'I know. I went out.'

'So I was told. I—suppose you wouldn't consider joining me for some coffee?' she asked.

He gave another grunt. 'Sure you can trust me?'

Lucille made no reply to this. She thought privately that it was more likely to be herself she could not trust.

Blair said as they went up in the lift, 'I want to talk to you anyway, so a chat over a cup of coffee would be a good idea.'

He rang down himself and ordered it, and while they were waiting for it to be brought, he took her arm and propelled her out on to the balcony.

'Take a look at that,' he said, indicating the panorama below.

Lucille looked, and gave a gasp of sheer delight and wonderment.

'Oh! Oh, my goodness—how beautiful, how absolutely wonderful!'

She could scarely believe her eyes, had never thought she would see a sight so lovely and so exciting. It was now quite dark, and through the soft blackness was pricked out a thousand multi-coloured lights, diamond clusters of the villages, down, down and all around. No buildings showed, no floodlights, just a glorious panorama of different coloured lights on which to feast one's eyes. Lucille found herself so deeply moved she almost wanted to weep. She sought Blair's hand and felt she would die if he repulsed her. But his hand enfolded hers briefly before he said, 'Let's go in now. The coffee has arrived.'

Reluctantly, she followed back into the room where the waiter had placed the tray of coffee on a low table. Lucille sat down in one of the elegant armchairs to pour it, and Blair sat opposite her. As she poured the coffee, she felt his gaze upon her, and her hands began to tremble.

'What—what was it you wanted to talk to me about?' she asked.

'I want to talk to you about the future,' he said without looking at her.

She frowned. 'What do you mean—the future? You promised me I should have my old job back at the London hotel.'

'I know, but I have another one to offer you.'

'What sort of job? I don't want to be anyone's secretary.'

'That's not what I had in mind.' He looked at her then, and she loved him so much she wanted with all her heart to cross over to him, to lean her head on his knee, to feel his fingers through her hair.

'Then—then what had you in mind?' she asked, sipping nervously at her coffee.

'A job as my personal assistant.'

Lucille shook her head vigorously. She couldn't. It was impossible. She just wouldn't be able to bear working so closely with him feeling as she did. The sooner she was back in London in her own flat, the sooner she could set about trying to forget him.

'No. No, I can't,' she forced out, finding her voice at last.

'Why not?' he asked, giving her a steady look. 'Anything to do with your boyfriend, Jim?'

She stared at him wide-eyed. 'With Jim? No, of course not. It's—it's just that you and I—I mean, we—don't seem to get along together all that well. You—you've cut short this six-month project. I really don't see now why you want to change your mind.'

She was having great difficulty in keeping her voice steady. The strain and tension since she had known she was in love with Blair were at breaking point. She wished he would go, but his coffee remained on the table untouched. She could feel something uncontrollable welling up inside her. Had it been his room they were in she would have got up and left.

'I haven't necessarily changed my mind about this project,' he told her quietly.

'Then—then what? I do wish to goodness you'd make yourself clear!' The words came out in a half sob. The cup in her hand from which she had been making a pretence of drinking rattled in its saucer, and she put it down on the table with a hand that shook. She put the hand to her mouth in a tremendous effort to keep control of her emotions. How could she keep on working with Blair as his assistant, whatever new idea he had in his mind? She simply couldn't.

'Come here,' he demanded suddenly.

She looked at him uncertainly, but he gestured to her to come over to him.

'But—but why?' she asked wildly. She did not want him to touch her; she would much rather she stayed where she was.

'Do as you're told and come over here,' he reiterated.

There was something in the tone of his voice which brooked no opposition. Reluctantly, yet with a feeling that she simply must do as he asked, Lucille rose slowly to her feet and crossed over to where he was sitting.

To her utter astonishment he reached out and pulled her on to his knee. The next moment he had his arms tightly around her and was kissing her in the same passionate, hungry way he had in the taxi in Paris. The whole of that evening flashed through her mind, and she struggled against him. She did not want this, she wanted him to love her, not simply desire her. But her struggles were in vain, and as his kisses became more and more possessive she found her resistance weakening.

With a half-sob she gave herself up to him. Her arms went around his neck and with sudden passion she pressed herself closer to him.

'Blair—oh, Blair!'

She clung to him, returning kiss for kiss, no longer caring about anything except that she was in his arms.

'Lucille,' she heard him murmur in a broken voice. 'I love you, I love you, I love you——'

'Blair, you can't, you don't mean it. Please, please don't say things you don't mean!'

At this he grasped her by the shoulders and looked at her, an expression on his face she had never dreamed she would ever see there. It was one full of tenderness and wonder. His glance flicked over her every feature and he ran the back of his hand softly down her cheek.

'Don't mean it? What do I have to say, what do I have to do to convince you? Why do you think you're here? I didn't have to bring you on this trip—I could have chosen any one of those girls I interviewed that evening when I first met you. In fact, I wasn't interviewing any of them for this. I wanted a secretary for one of my other hotels—a new one near Gatwick. It opens in two weeks' time.'

Lucille gave him a puzzled look. 'But—but I don't understand. Why did you bring me here if you didn't need someone?'

He laughed shortly. 'I needed *you*. I fell in love with you the minute I set eyes on you, and I meant to have you.'

'To—to have me?' she repeated stupidly. She couldn't believe what was happening, that he was serious. It all seemed too incredible.

'Yes, to have you,' he asserted, in a voice that reached down to the very core of her being.

'Then—then why did you want to cut short this trip? Why did you begin to make love to me that night in Paris and then leave me?'

Blair's eyes widened. 'Did you want me to go on?' he asked softly.

'I—I don't know,' she answered in confusion.

His eyes narrowed, and he gripped her shoulders so tightly that it hurt.

'My dear, darling girl, you'll never know what it cost me to get so far and then leave you.'

Tears welled up in her eyes. 'You—could have done absolutely anything you wanted. If you'd asked me to stand on my head, I would have.'

'Why, Lucille? Why would you?'

She put her hand to her head, trying to think back. 'I—I don't know. It must have been because I——' She broke off. She had not, at that time, known that she loved him.

'Lucille,' he said earnestly. 'Lucille, do you love me? Do you think you could ever love me?'

She stared at him. 'But of course I love you!' she exclaimed on a note of exasperation.

Blair began to laugh. 'There's no "of course" about it. You've been the most moody, difficult, off-putting woman I've ever met in my life—and I've met some.'

'So I've heard!' she retorted.

'Oh, you've heard, have you? From whom, may I ask?'

'I'm *not* going to tell you,' she retorted. 'Anyway, isn't it true? What about that woman you kept ringing at different hotels, and who rang you?'

He laughed again. 'That, my darling, believe it or not, was my mother.'

'Then why didn't you say so?'

'Didn't I? I thought I had,' he said with bland innocence.

'You know perfectly well you didn't! And talk about me being difficult! You insisted on my not phoning my friends——'

'Such as that Jim fellow——'

'Yes, such as Jim. Then you were downright rude to him, and to me, when he dared to ring me.'

'Naturally,' drawled Blair.

'You got annoyed about that man Timothy Collins, poor harmless soul.'

'Harmless my foot!'

'And yet you were with some woman in Amsterdam. We saw you.'

His eyebrows lifted. 'You did?'

'Yes, I did.'

'And you were jealous. Come on, now, admit it!'

She looked at him and gave a little laugh. 'Yes, I expect I was.' Then she laughed out of sheer happiness, still feeling a sense of unreality about it all. 'How extraordinary it is! Yes, I suppose I was jealous, though I didn't realise it at the time.'

'And I was as jealous as hell about that fellow Jim. Why do you think I insisted on "six months' uninterrupted work with no distractions"? I was determined to win you, but I knew it wasn't going to be easy. It was clear all along that you were a woman who knew her own mind. I thought I needed six months to get to work on you.' Still keeping a firm hold on her, Blair leaned back in his chair and sighed. 'Oh, that night in Paris! You looked so wonderful, I could hardly keep my hands off you. In fact, in the end I couldn't resist you. You responded to me in the taxi, but I couldn't believe it was because you loved me. And then when I unzipped your dress——' He closed his eyes for a moment, an ecstatic look on his face. 'Darling, you were absolutely wonderful! I knew you'd reached the stage when you probably wouldn't resist me. But partly because I thought you might well push me away at some stage, and that I couldn't have taken, and partly because I wanted to wait until I'd really won your love, I stopped short.'

'You called me a prude!' Lucille said accusingly.

'So I did. And so you were, and darling, so was I, really. I didn't want you on the cheap, tempting though you were. You have the most beautiful shoulders I've ever seen on any woman. And then, it seemed, you ran away from me at every turn.'

She bent over and kissed his cheek and felt him tremble. 'I was afraid. I knew that you only had to touch me and I was lost.'

He gave her a long, devouring look. 'And how do you feel at this moment?'

She smoothed back his hair. 'I want this moment, this time and this place to last for ever. I want time to stand still. I feel as though I'm going to burst any minute, I'm so happy.'

Blair's arms tightened around her. 'I want to eat you. And to think I nearly lost you in that damned fire!' He shuddered. 'I've never been so near to going out of my mind in my whole life! My only thought was to get to you. If you were—dead, then I'd want to die too. You can't imagine the heavenly relief when I found you were still alive. And to think, too, that I was jealous of David. Which reminds me, I understand he asked you to marry him.'

Lucille laughed. 'He wasn't serious.'

'He was. I tell you, you've given me more trouble than a whole cartload of women! And then,' he added indignantly, 'you were dead scared that I wanted to share this suite with you.'

'Well, of course I was, although I took it for granted before we got here that *you* were going to have the suite— as befits the boss. And I was going to have the single room. And then you went out and left me!'

'I didn't know what to do with myself, I loved you so much. I thought it was hopeless.'

'And you were ready to give in?'

'Almost. I didn't want to force you, and I was so damned unsure, in spite of what David said.'

Her mind alerted. 'And what did David say, may I ask?'

'I'll tell you. He said, "Why don't you ask that girl to marry you?" I answered, "She wouldn't have me. She runs a mile if I as much as try to touch her".'

'And what did David say to that, for goodness' sake?'

'He said, "You're a blithering idiot".'

Lucille grinned. 'I think I agree with him.'

Blair gave her a threatening look. 'Oh, do you?'

'Yes. And are you going to take his advice? Are you going to ask me to marry you?'

'But I have!'

'Oh, no, you haven't.'

He grabbed her hair from the back and brought her face down to his. 'Do you need to be asked, you little idiot? Of course I want you to marry me. Will you?'

She laughed at the hint of anxiety in his voice. She was so happy, she still couldn't believe it.

She brought her lips slowly down on his and kissed him. 'I'll think about it,' she murmured.

'You'll do more than think about it,' he muttered.

Teasingly she wrenched herself away from him with a suddenness which so took him by surprise that she was free in an instant.

'About that job you offered me,' she mused. 'Your personal assistant. I think I'll take it.'

Blair leapt out of the chair and she pretended to run away from him again, going out on to the balcony. She stood there for a moment, then she felt his arms come around her from the back and hold her. She leaned her head back on to his shoulder.

He kissed the lobe of her ear. 'Shall I tell you something? I planned to ask you to marry me here, in this room, on this balcony. This was going to be our last port of call in six months' time, and in this suite we'll spend our honeymoon. Do you like the idea?'

'I love it.'

For a few moments they stood there, gazing at the beautiful panorama of lights, drinking in the peace which might have lasted for an eternity. Then Blair took her hand and led her indoors again. Lucille could feel him trembling, and when he put both his hands on her shoulders, her whole being surged towards him.

'Darling,' he said, in a carefully controlled voice, 'I love you so much.' Slowly he pulled her towards him. 'Shall I go? Ought I to go? Or would you like me to stay?'

Afraid no longer, she ran the back of her fingers down his face.

'Stay, Blair, stay,' she murmured softly.

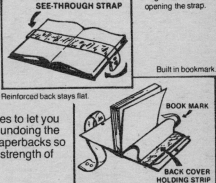

Keepsake